Douglas Adams created all the various and contradictory manifestations of *The Hitchhiker's Guide to the Galaxy*: radio, novels, TV, computer game, stage adaptations, comic book and bath towel. A major movie is currently in development hell and will almost certainly be released any decade now. He lectured and broadcast around the world and was a patron of the Dian Fossey Gorilla Fund and Save the Rhino International.

He was born in Cambridge, UK and lived with his wife and daughter in Santa Barbara, California, where he died suddenly on 11 May 2001.

For more information, visit *www.douglasadams.com*

If you are interested in the works of Douglas Adams, you may like to join ZZ9 Plural Z Alpha, the official Hitchhiker's Guide to the Galaxy Appreciation Society, founded in 1980. For details of this fan-run club visit www.zz9.org or send a SAE/IRC to:

ZZ9 Plural Z Alpha
4 The Sycamores, Hadfield
Derbyshire, SK13 2BS, UK

by the same author

The Hitchhiker series:

The Hitchhiker's Guide to the Galaxy
The Restaurant at the End of the Universe
Life, the Universe and Everything
So Long, and Thanks for all the Fish
Mostly Harmless

The Dirk Gently series:

Dirk Gently's Holistic Detective Agency
The Long Dark Tea-time of the Soul

With John Lloyd:

The Meaning of Liff
The Deeper Meaning of Liff

With Mark Carwardine:

Last Chance to See . . .

By Terry Jones, based on a story/
computer game by Douglas Adams:

Starship Titanic

DOUGLAS ADAMS

The Restaurant at the End of the Universe

Pan Books

First published 1980 by Pan Books
an imprint of Pan Macmillan Ltd
Pan Macmillan, 20 New Wharf Road, London N1 9RR
Basingstoke and Oxford
Associated companies throughout the world
www.panmacmillan.com

ISBN-13: 978-0330-26213-2
ISBN-10: 0-330-26213-0

69

A CIP catalogue record for this book is available from the British Library.

Typeset by SetSystems Ltd, Saffron Walden, Essex
Printed and bound in Great Britain by
Mackays of Chatham plc, Chatham, Kent

To Jane and James

with many thanks

to Geoffrey Perkins for achieving the Improbable

to Paddy Kingsland, Lisa Braun and
Alick Hale Munro for helping him

to John Lloyd for his help with the
original Milliways script

to Simon Brett for starting the whole thing off

to the Paul Simon album *One Trick Pony* which
I played incessantly while writing this book.
Five years is far too long

And with very special thanks to
Jacqui Graham for infinite patience,
kindness and food in adversity

There is a theory which states that if ever
anyone discovers exactly what the Universe
is for and why it is here, it will instantly
disappear and be replaced by something
even more bizarre and inexplicable.

There is another theory which states
that this has already happened.

1

The story so far:

In the beginning the Universe was created.

This had made a lot of people very angry and been widely regarded as a bad move.

Many races believe that it was created by some sort of god, though the Jatravartid people of Viltvodle Six believe that the entire Universe was in fact sneezed out of the nose of a being called the Great Green Arkleseizure.

The Jatravartids, who live in perpetual fear of the time they call the Coming of the Great White Handkerchief, are small blue creatures with more than fifty arms each, who are therefore unique in being the only race in history to have invented the aerosol deodorant before the wheel.

However, the Great Green Arkleseizure Theory is not widely accepted outside Viltvodle Six and so, the Universe being the puzzling place it is, other explanations are constantly being sought.

For instance, a race of hyper-intelligent pan-dimensional beings once built themselves a gigantic supercomputer called Deep Thought to calculate once and for all the Answer to the Ultimate Question of Life, the Universe and Everything.

For seven and a half million years, Deep Thought computed and calculated, and in the end announced that the answer was in fact Forty-two – and so another, even bigger, computer had to be built to find out what the actual question was.

And this computer, which was called the Earth, was so large that it was frequently mistaken for a planet – especially by the strange ape-like beings who roamed its surface, totally unaware that they were simply part of a gigantic computer program.

And this is very odd, because without that fairly simple and obvious piece of knowledge, nothing that ever happened on the Earth could possibly make the slightest bit of sense.

Sadly, however, just before the critical moment of readout, the Earth was unexpectedly demolished by the Vogons to make way – so they claimed – for a new hyperspace bypass, and so all hope of discovering a meaning for life was lost for ever.

Or so it would seem.

Two of these strange, ape-like creatures survived.

Arthur Dent escaped at the very last moment because an old friend of his, Ford Prefect, suddenly turned out to be from a small planet somewhere in the vicinity of Betelgeuse and not from Guildford as he had hitherto claimed; and, more to the point, he knew how to hitch rides on flying saucers.

Tricia McMillan – or Trillian – had skipped the planet six months earlier with Zaphod Beeblebrox, the then President of the Galaxy.

Two survivors.

They are all that remains of the greatest experiment ever conducted – to find the Ultimate Question and the Ultimate Answer of Life, the Universe and Everything.

And, less than half a million miles from where their starship is drifting lazily through the inky blackness of space, a Vogon ship is moving slowly towards them.

2

Like all Vogon ships it looked as if it had been not so much designed as congealed. The unpleasant yellow lumps and edifices which protruded from it at unsightly angles would have disfigured the looks of most ships, but in this case that was sadly impossible. Uglier things have been spotted in the skies, but not by reliable witnesses.

In fact to see anything much uglier than a Vogon ship you would have to go inside it and look at a Vogon. If you are wise, however, this is precisely what you will avoid doing because the average Vogon will not think twice before doing something so pointlessly hideous to you that you will wish you had never been born – or (if you are a clearer minded thinker) that the Vogon had never been born.

In fact, the average Vogon probably wouldn't even think once. They are simple-minded, thick-willed, slug-brained creatures, and thinking is not really something they are cut out for. Anatomical analysis of the Vogon reveals that its brain was originally a badly deformed, misplaced and dyspeptic liver. The fairest thing you can say about them, then, is that they know what they like, and what they like generally involves hurting people and, wherever possible, getting very angry.

One thing they don't like is leaving a job unfinished – particularly this Vogon, and particularly – for various reasons – this job.

This Vogon was Captain Prostetnic Vogon Jeltz of the Galactic Hyperspace Planning Council, and he it was who had had the job of demolishing the so-called 'planet' Earth.

He heaved his monumentally vile body round in his ill-fitting, slimy seat and stared at the monitor screen on which the starship *Heart of Gold* was being systematically scanned.

It mattered little to him that the *Heart of Gold*, with its Infinite Improbability Drive, was the most beautiful and revolutionary ship ever built. Aesthetics and technology were closed books to him and, had he had his way, burnt and buried books as well.

It mattered even less to him that Zaphod Beeblebrox was aboard. Zaphod Beeblebrox was now the ex-President of the Galaxy, and though every police force in the Galaxy was currently pursuing both him and this ship he had stolen, the Vogon was not interested.

He had other fish to fry.

It has been said that Vogons are not above a little bribery and corruption in the same way that the sea is not above the clouds, and this was certainly true in his case. When he heard the words 'integrity' or 'moral rectitude' he reached for his dictionary, and when he heard the chink of ready money in large quantities he reached for the rule book and threw it away.

In seeking so implacably the destruction of the Earth and all that therein lay he was moving somewhat above and beyond the call of his professional duty. There was even some doubt as to whether the said bypass was actually going to be built, but the matter had been glossed over.

He grunted a repellent grunt of satisfaction.

'Computer,' he croaked, 'get me my brain-care specialist on the line.'

Within a few seconds the face of Gag Halfrunt appeared on the screen, smiling the smile of a man who knew he was ten light-years away from the Vogon face he was looking at. Mixed up somewhere in the smile was a glint of irony too. Though the Vogon persistently referred to him as 'my private brain-care specialist' there was not a lot of brain to take care of, and it was in fact Halfrunt who was employing the Vogon. He was paying him an awful lot of money to do some very dirty work. As one of the Galaxy's most prominent and successful psychiatrists, he and a consortium of his colleagues were quite prepared to spend an awful lot of money when it seemed that the entire future of psychiatry might be at stake.

'Well,' he said, 'hello my Captain of Vogons Prostetnic, and how are we feeling today?'

The Vogon Captain told him that in the last few hours he had wiped out nearly half his crew in a disciplinary exercise.

Halfrunt's smile did not flicker for an instant.

'Well,' he said. 'I think this is perfectly normal behaviour for a Vogon, you know? The natural and healthy channelling of the aggressive instincts into acts of senseless violence.'

'That,' rumbled the Vogon, 'is what you always say.'

'Well again,' said Halfrunt, 'I think that this is perfectly normal behaviour for a psychiatrist. Good. We are clearly both very well adjusted in our mental attitudes today. Now tell me, what news of the mission?'

'We have located the ship.'

'Wonderful,' said Halfrunt, 'wonderful! And the occupants?'

'The Earthman is there.'

'Excellent! And . . .?'

'A female from the same planet. They are the last.'

'Good, good,' beamed Halfrunt, 'Who else?'

'The man Prefect.'

'Yes?'

'And Zaphod Beeblebrox.'

For an instant Halfrunt's smile flickered.

'Ah yes,' he said, 'I had been expecting this. It is most regrettable.'

'A personal friend?' enquired the Vogon, who had heard the expression somewhere once and decided to try it out.

'Ah, no,' said Halfrunt, 'in my profession you know, we do not make personal friends.'

'Ah,' grunted the Vogon, 'professional detachment.'

'No,' said Halfrunt cheerfully 'we just don't have the knack.'

He paused. His mouth continued to smile, but his eyes frowned slightly.

'But Beeblebrox, you know,' he said, 'he is one of my most profitable clients. He has personality problems beyond the dreams of analysts.'

He toyed with this thought a little before reluctantly dismissing it.

'Still,' he said, 'you are ready for your task?'

'Yes.'

'Good. Destroy the ship immediately.'

'What about Beeblebrox?'

'Well,' said Halfrunt brightly, 'Zaphod's just this guy, you know?'

He vanished from the screen.

The Vogon captain pressed a communicator button which connected him with the remains of his crew.

'Attack,' he said.

At that precise moment Zaphod Beeblebrox was in his cabin swearing very loudly. Two hours ago, he had said that they would go for a quick bite at the Restaurant at the End of the Universe, whereupon he had had a blazing row with the ship's computer and stormed off to his cabin shouting that he would work out the Improbability factors with a pencil.

The *Heart of Gold*'s Improbability Drive made it the most powerful and unpredictable ship in existence. There was nothing it couldn't do, provided you knew exactly how improbable it was that the thing you wanted it to do would ever happen.

He had stolen it when, as President, he was meant to be launching it. He didn't know exactly why he had stolen it, except that he liked it.

He didn't know why he had become President of the Galaxy, except that it seemed a fun thing to be.

He did know that there were better reasons than these, but that they were buried in a dark, locked-off section of his two brains. He wished the dark, locked-off section of his two brains would go away because they occasionally surfaced momentarily and put strange thoughts into the light, fun sections of his mind and tried to deflect him from what he saw as being the basic business of his life, which was to have a wonderfully good time.

At the moment he was not having a wonderfully good time. He had run out of patience and pencils and was feeling very hungry.

'Starpox!' he shouted.

At that same precise moment, Ford Prefect was in mid-air. This was not because of anything wrong with the ship's artificial gravity field, but because he was leaping down the stairwell which led to the ship's personal cabins. It was a very high jump to do in one bound and he landed awkwardly, stumbled, recovered, raced down the corridor sending a couple of miniature service robots flying, skidded round the corner, burst into Zaphod's door and explained what was on his mind.

'Vogons,' he said.

A short while before this, Arthur Dent had set out from his cabin in search of a cup of tea. It was not a quest he embarked upon with a great deal of optimism, because he knew that the only source of hot drinks on the entire ship was a benighted piece of equipment produced by the Sirius Cybernetics Corporation. It was called a Nutri-Matic Drinks Synthesizer, and he had encountered it before.

It claimed to produce the widest possible range of drinks personally matched to the tastes and metabolism of whoever cared to use it. When put to the test, however, it invariably produced a plastic cup filled with a liquid which was almost, but not quite, entirely unlike tea.

He attempted to reason with the thing.

'Tea,' he said.

'Share and Enjoy,' the machine repeated and produced another one.

'Share and Enjoy' is the company motto of the hugely successful Sirius Cybernetics Corporation Complaints division, which now covers the major land masses of three medium-sized planets and is the only part of the Corporation to have shown a consistent profit in recent years.

The motto stands – or rather stood – in three-mile high illuminated letters near the Complaints Department spaceport on Eadraz. Unfortunately its weight was such that shortly after it was erected, the ground beneath the letters caved in and they dropped for nearly half their length through the offices of many talented young complaints executives – now deceased.

The protruding upper halves of the letters now appear, in the local language, to read 'Go stick your head in a pig', and are no longer illuminated, except at times of special celebration.

Arthur threw away a sixth cup of the liquid.

'Listen, you machine,' he said, 'you claim you can synthesize any drink in existence, so why do you keep giving me the same undrinkable stuff?'

'Nutrition and pleasurable sense data,' burbled the machine, 'Share and Enjoy.'

'It tastes filthy!'

'If you have enjoyed the experience of this drink,' continued the machine, 'why not share it with your friends?'

'Because,' said Arthur tartly, 'I want to keep them. Will you try to comprehend what I'm telling you? That drink . . .'

'That drink,' said the machine sweetly, 'was individually tailored to meet your personal requirements for nutrition and pleasure.'

'Ah,' said Arthur, 'so I'm a masochist on a diet, am I?'

'Share and Enjoy.'

'Oh shut up.'

'Will that be all?'

Arthur decided to give up.

'Yes,' he said.

Then he decided he'd be damned if he'd give up.

'No,' he said, 'look, it's very, very simple . . . all I want . . . is a cup of tea. You are going to make one for me. Keep quiet and listen.'

And he sat. He told the Nutri-Matic about India, he told it about China, he told it about Ceylon. He told it about broad leaves drying in the sun. He told it about silver teapots. He told it about summer afternoons on the lawn. He told it about putting in the milk before the tea so it wouldn't get scalded. He even told it (briefly) about the history of the East India Company.

'So that's it, is it?' said the Nutri-Matic when he had finished.

'Yes,' said Arthur, 'that is what I want.'

'You want the taste of dried leaves boiled in water?'

'Er, yes. With milk.'

'Squirted out of a cow?'

'Well, in a manner of speaking I suppose . . .'

'I'm going to need some help with this one,' said the machine tersely. All the cheerful burbling had dropped out of its voice and it now meant business.

'Well, anything I can do,' said Arthur.

'You've done quite enough,' the Nutri-Matic informed him.

It summoned up the ship's computer.

'Hi there!' said the ship's computer.

The Nutri-Matic explained about tea to the ship's computer. The computer boggled, linked logic circuits with the Nutri-Matic and together they lapsed into a grim silence.

Arthur watched and waited for a while, but nothing further happened.

He thumped it, but still nothing happened.

Eventually he gave up and wandered up to the bridge.

In the empty wastes of space, the *Heart of Gold* hung still. Around it blazed the billion pinpricks of the Galaxy. Towards it crept the ugly yellow lump of the Vogon ship.

3

'Does anyone have a kettle?' Arthur asked as he walked on to the bridge, and instantly began to wonder why Trillian was yelling at the computer to talk to her, Ford was thumping it and Zaphod was kicking it, and also why there was a nasty yellow lump on the vision screen.

He put down the empty cup he was carrying and walked over to them.

'Hello?' he said.

At that moment Zaphod flung himself over to the polished marble surface that contained the instruments that controlled the conventional photon drive. They materialized beneath his hands and he flipped over to manual control. He pushed, he pulled, he pressed and he swore. The photon drive gave a sickly judder and cut out again.

'Something up?' said Arthur.

'Hey, didja hear that,' muttered Zaphod as he leapt now for the manual controls on the Infinite Improbability Drive, 'the monkey spoke!'

The Improbability Drive gave two small whines and then also cut out.

'Pure history, man,' said Zaphod, kicking the Improbability Drive, 'a talking monkey!'

'If you're upset about something . . .' said Arthur.

'Vogons!' snapped Ford. 'We're under attack!'

Arthur gibbered.

'Well what are you doing? Let's get out of here!'

'Can't. Computer's jammed.'

'Jammed?'

'It says all its circuits are occupied. There's no power anywhere in the ship.'

Ford moved away from the computer terminal, wiped a sleeve across his forehead and slumped back against the wall.

'Nothing we can do,' he said. He glared at nothing and bit his lip.

When Arthur had been a boy at school, long before the Earth had been demolished, he had used to play football. He had not been at all good at it, and his particular speciality had been scoring own goals in important matches. Whenever this happened he used to experience a peculiar tingling round the back of his neck that would slowly creep up across his cheeks and heat his brow. The image of mud and grass and lots of little jeering boys flinging it at him suddenly came vividly to his mind at this moment.

A peculiar tingling sensation at the back of his neck was creeping up across his cheeks and heating his brow.

He started to speak, and stopped.

He started to speak again and stopped again.

Finally he managed to speak.

'Er,' he said. He cleared his throat.

'Tell me,' he continued, and said it so nervously that the others all turned to stare at him. He glanced at the approaching yellow blob on the vision screen.

'Tell me,' he said again, 'did the computer say what was occupying it? I just ask out of interest . . .'

Their eyes were riveted on him.

'And, er . . . well that's it really, just asking.'

Zaphod put out a hand and held Arthur by the scruff of the neck.

'What have you done to it, Monkeyman?' he breathed.

'Well,' said Arthur, 'nothing in fact. It's just that I think a short while ago it was trying to work out how to . . .'

'Yes?'

'Make me some tea.'

'That's right, guys,' the computer sang out suddenly, 'just coping with that problem right now, and wow, it's a biggy. Be with you in a while.' It lapsed back into a silence that was only matched for sheer intensity by the silence of the three people staring at Arthur Dent.

As if to relieve the tension, the Vogons chose that moment to start firing.

The ship shook, the ship thundered. Outside, the inch-thick force-shield around it blistered, crackled and spat under the barrage of a dozen 30-Megahurt Definit-Kil Photrazon Cannon, and looked as if it wouldn't be around for long. Four minutes is how long Ford Prefect gave it.

'Three minutes and fifty seconds,' he said a short while later.

'Forty-five seconds,' he added at the appropriate time. He flicked idly at some useless switches, then gave Arthur an unfriendly look.

'Dying for a cup of tea, eh?' he said. 'Three minutes and forty seconds.'

'Will you stop counting!' snarled Zaphod.

'Yes,' said Ford Prefect, 'in three minutes and thirty-five seconds.'

Aboard the Vogon ship, Prostetnic Vogon Jeltz was puzzled. He had expected a chase, he had expected an exciting grapple with tractor beams, he had expected to have to use the specially installed Sub-Cyclic Normality Assert-i-Tron to counter the *Heart of Gold*'s Infinite Improbability Drive; but the Sub-Cyclic Normality Assert-i-Tron lay idle as the *Heart of Gold* just sat there and took it.

A dozen 30-Megahurt Definit-Kil Photrazon Cannon continued to blaze away at the *Heart of Gold*, and still it just sat there and took it.

He tested every sensor at his disposal to see if there was any subtle trickery afoot, but no subtle trickery was to be found.

He didn't know about the tea, of course.

Nor did he know exactly how the occupants of the *Heart of Gold* were spending the last three minutes and thirty seconds of life they had left to spend.

Quite how Zaphod Beeblebrox arrived at the idea of holding a seance at this point is something he was never quite clear on.

Obviously the subject of death was in the air, but more as something to be avoided than harped upon.

Possibly the horror that Zaphod experienced at the prospect of being reunited with his deceased relatives led on to the thought that they might just feel the same way about him and, what's more, be able to do something about helping to postpone this reunion.

Or again it might just have been one of the strange promptings that occasionally surfaced from that dark area of his mind that he had inexplicably locked off prior to becoming President of the Galaxy.

'You want to talk to your great-grandfather?' boggled Ford.

'Yeah.'

'Does it have to be *now*?'

The ship continued to shake and thunder. The temperature was rising. The light was getting dimmer – all the energy the computer didn't require for thinking about tea was being pumped into the rapidly fading force-field.

'Yeah!' insisted Zaphod. 'Listen, Ford, I think he may be able to help us.'

'Are you sure you mean *think*? Pick your words with care.'

'Suggest something else we can do.'

'Er, well . . .'

'OK, round the central console. Now. Come on! Trillian, Monkeyman, move.'

They clustered round the central console in confusion, sat down and, feeling exceptionally foolish, held hands. With his third hand Zaphod turned off the lights.

Darkness grabbed the ship.

Outside, the thunderous roar of the Definit-Kil cannon continued to rip at the force-field.

'Concentrate,' hissed Zaphod, 'on his name.'

'What is it?' asked Arthur.

'Zaphod Beeblebrox the Fourth.'

'What?'

'Zaphod Beeblebrox the Fourth, Concentrate!'

'The Fourth?'

'Yeah. Listen, I'm Zaphod Beeblebrox, my father was

Zaphod Beeblebrox the Second, my grandfather Zaphod Beeblebrox the Third . . .'

'What?'

'There was an accident with a contraceptive and a time machine. Now concentrate!'

'Three minutes,' said Ford Prefect.

'Why,' said Arthur Dent, 'are we doing this?'

'Shut up,' suggested Zaphod Beeblebrox.

Trillian said nothing. What, she thought, was there to say?

The only light on the bridge came from two dim red triangles in a far corner where Marvin the Paranoid Android sat slumped, ignoring all and ignored by all, in a private and rather unpleasant world of his own.

Round the central console four figures hunched in tight concentration trying to blot from their minds the terrifying shuddering of the ship and the fearful roar that echoed through it.

They concentrated.

Still they concentrated.

And still they concentrated.

The seconds ticked by.

On Zaphod's brows stood beads of sweat, first of concentration, then of frustration and finally of embarrassment.

At last he let out a cry of anger, snatched back his hands from Trillian and Ford and stabbed at the light switch.

'Ah, I was beginning to think you'd never turn the lights on,' said a voice. 'No, not too bright please, my eyes aren't what they once were.'

Four figures jolted upright in their seats. Slowly they turned their heads to look, though their scalps showed a distinct propensity to try and stay in the same place.

'Now. Who disturbs me at this time?' said the small, bent, gaunt figure standing by the sprays of fern at the far end of the bridge. His two small wispy-haired heads looked so ancient that it seemed they might hold dim memories of the birth of the galaxies themselves. One lolled in sleep, the other squinted sharply at them. If his eyes weren't what they once were, they must once have been diamond cutters.

Zaphod stuttered nervously for a moment. He gave the intricate little double nod which is the traditional Betelgeusian gesture of familiar respect.

'Oh . . . er, hi, Great-grandad . . .' he breathed.

The little old figure moved closer towards them. He peered through the dim light. He thrust out a bony finger at his great grandson.

'Ah,' he snapped, 'Zaphod Beeblebrox. The last of our great line. Zaphod Beeblebrox the Nothingth.'

'The First.'

'The Nothingth,' spat the figure. Zaphod hated his voice. It always seemed to him to screech like fingernails across the blackboard of what he liked to think of as his soul.

He shifted awkwardly in his seat.

'Er, yeah,' he muttered. 'Er, look, I'm really sorry about the flowers, I meant to send them along, but you know, the shop was fresh out of wreaths and . . .'

'You forgot!' snapped Zaphod Beeblebrox the Fourth.

'Well . . .'

'Too busy. Never think of other people. The living are all the same.'

'Two minutes, Zaphod,' whispered Ford in an awed whisper.

Zaphod fidgeted nervously.

'Yeah, but I did mean to send them,' he said. 'And I'll write to my great-grandmother as well, just as soon as we get out of this . . .'

'Your great-grandmother,' mused the gaunt little figure to himself.

'Yeah,' said Zaphod. 'Er, how is she? Tell you what, I'll go and see her. But first we've just got to . . .'

'Your *late* great-grandmother and I are very well,' rasped Zaphod Beeblebrox the Fourth.

'Ah. Oh.'

'But very disappointed in you, young Zaphod . . .'

'Yeah, well . . .' Zaphod felt strangely powerless to take charge of this conversation, and Ford's heavy breathing at his side told him that the seconds were ticking away fast. The noise and the shaking had reached terrifying proportions. He saw Trillian and Arthur's faces white and unblinking in the gloom.

'Er, Great-grandfather . . .'

'We've been following your progress with considerable despondency . . .'

'Yeah, look, just at the moment, you see . . .'

'Not to say contempt!'

'Could you sort of listen for a moment . . .'

'I mean what exactly are you doing with your life?'

'I'm being attacked by a Vogon fleet!' cried Zaphod. It was an exaggeration, but it was his only opportunity so far of getting the basic point of the exercise across.

'Doesn't surprise me in the least,' said the little old figure with a shrug.

'Only it's happening right now, you see,' insisted Zaphod feverishly.

The spectral ancestor nodded, picked up the cup Arthur Dent had brought in and looked at it with interest.

'Er . . . Great-grandad . . .'

'Did you know,' interrupted the ghostly figure, fixing Zaphod with a stern look, 'that Betelgeuse Five has now developed a very slight eccentricity in its orbit?'

Zaphod didn't and found the information hard to concentrate on what with all the noise and the imminence of death and so on.

'Er, no . . . look,' he said.

'Me spinning in my grave!' barked the ancestor. He

slammed the cup down and pointed a quivering, stick-like see-through finger at Zaphod.

'Your fault!' he screeched.

'One minute thirty,' muttered Ford, his head in his hands.

'Yeah, look Great-grandad, can you actually, help because . . .'

'Help?' exclaimed the old man as if he'd been asked for a stoat.

'Yeah, help, and like, now, because otherwise . . .'

'Help!' repeated the old man as if he'd been asked for a lightly grilled stoat in a bun with French fries. He stood amazed.

'You go swanning your way round the Galaxy with your . . .' the ancestor waved a contemptuous hand, 'with your disreputable friends, too busy to put flowers on my grave, plastic ones would have done, would have been quite appropriate from you, but no. Too busy. Too modern. Too sceptical – till you suddenly find yourself in a bit of a fix and come over suddenly all astrally-minded!'

He shook his head – carefully, so as not to disturb the slumber of the other one, which was already becoming restive.

'Well, I don't know, young Zaphod,' he continued, 'I think I'll have to think about this one.'

'One minute ten,' said Ford hollowly.

Zaphod Beeblebrox the Fourth peered at him curiously.

'Why does that man keep talking in numbers?' he said.

'Those numbers,' said Zaphod tersely, 'are the time we've got left to live.'

'Oh,' said his great-grandfather. He grunted to himself. 'Doesn't apply to me, of course,' he said and moved off to a dimmer recess of the bridge in search of something else to poke around at.

Zaphod felt he was teetering on the edge of madness and wondered if he shouldn't just jump over and have done with it.

'Great-grandfather,' he said, 'it applies to us! We are still alive, and we are about to lose our lives.'

'Good job too.'

'What?'

'What use is your life to anyone? When I think of what you've made of it the phrase "pig's ear" comes irresistibly to mind.'

'But I was President of the Galaxy, man!'

'Huh,' muttered his ancestor, 'and what kind of a job is that for a Beeblebrox?'

'Hey, what? Only President you know! Of the whole Galaxy!'

'Conceited little megapuppy.'

Zaphod blinked in bewilderment.

'Hey, er, what are you at, man? I mean Great-grandfather.'

The hunched up little figure stalked up to his great-grandson and tapped him sternly on the knee. This had the effect of reminding Zaphod that he was talking to a ghost because he didn't feel a thing.

'You know and I know what being President means, young Zaphod. You know because you've been it, and I know because I'm dead and it gives one such a wonderfully uncluttered perspective. We have a saying up here. "Life is wasted on the living."'

'Yeah,' said Zaphod bitterly, 'very good. Very deep. Right now I need aphorisms like I need holes in my heads.'

'Fifty seconds,' grunted Ford Prefect.

'Where was I?' said Zaphod Beeblebrox the Fourth.

'Pontificating,' said Zaphod Beeblebrox.

'Oh yes.'

'Can this guy,' muttered Ford quietly to Zaphod, 'actually in fact help us?'

'Nobody else can,' whispered Zaphod.

Ford nodded despondently.

'Zaphod,' the ghost was saying. 'You became President of the Galaxy for a reason. Have you forgotten?'

'Could we go into this later?'

'Have you forgotten?' insisted the ghost.

'Yeah! Of course I forgot! I had to forget. They screen your brain when you get the job, you know. If they'd found my head full of tricksy ideas I'd have been right out on the streets again with nothing but a fat pension, secretarial staff, a fleet of ships and a couple of slit throats.'

'Ah,' nodded the ghost in satisfaction, 'then you do remember!'

He paused for a moment.

'Good,' he said and the noise stopped.

'Forty-eight seconds,' said Ford. He looked again at his watch and tapped it. He looked up.

'Hey, the noise has stopped,' he said.

A mischievous twinkle gleamed in the ghost's hard little eyes.

'I've slowed down time for a moment,' he said, 'just for a moment, you understand. I would hate you to miss all I have to say.'

'No, you listen to me, you see-through old bat,' said Zaphod, leaping out of his chair, 'A – thanks for stopping time and all that, great, terrific, wonderful, but B – no thanks for the homily, right? I don't know what this great thing I'm meant to be doing is, and it looks to me as if I was supposed not to know. And I resent that, right?

'The old me knew. The old me cared. Fine, so far so

hoopy. Except that the old me cared so much that he actually got inside his own brain – my own brain – and locked off the bits that knew and cared, because if I knew and cared I wouldn't be able to do it. I wouldn't be able to go and be President, and I wouldn't be able to steal this ship, which must be the important thing.

'But this former self of mine killed himself off, didn't he, by changing my brain? OK, that was his choice. This new me has its own choices to make, and by a strange coincidence those choices involve not knowing and not caring about this big number, whatever it is. That's what he wanted, that's what he got.

'Except this old self of mine tried to leave himself in control, leaving orders for me in the bit of my brain he locked off. Well, I don't want to know, and I don't want to hear them. That's my choice. I'm not going to be anybody's puppet, particularly not my own.'

Zaphod banged on the console in fury, oblivious of the dumfounded looks he was attracting.

'The old me is dead!' he raved. 'Killed himself! The dead shouldn't hang about trying to interfere with the living!'

'And yet you summon me up to help you out of a scrape,' said the ghost.

'Ah,' said Zaphod, sitting down again, 'well that's different, isn't it?'

He grinned at Trillian, weakly.

'Zaphod,' rasped the apparition, 'I think the only reason I waste my breath on you is that being dead I don't have any other use for it.'

'OK,' said Zaphod, 'why don't you tell me what the big secret is. Try me.'

'Zaphod, you knew when you were President of the Galaxy, as did Yooden Vranx before you, that the President is nothing. A cipher. Somewhere in the shadows behind is another man, being, something, with ultimate power. That man, or being, or something, you must find – the man who controls this Galaxy, and – we suspect – others. Possibly the entire Universe.'

'Why?'

'Why?' exclaimed an astonished ghost, 'Why? Look around you lad, does it look to you as if it's in very good hands?'

'It's all right.'

The old ghost glowered at him.

'I will not argue with you. You will simply take this ship, this Improbability Drive ship, to where it is needed. You will do it. Don't think you can escape your purpose. The Improbability Field controls you, you are in its grip. What's this?'

He was standing tapping at one of the terminals of Eddie the Shipboard Computer. Zaphod told him.

'What's it doing?'

'It is trying,' said Zaphod with wonderful restraint, 'to make tea.'

'Good,' said his great-grandfather, 'I approve of that. Now, Zaphod,' he said, turning and wagging a finger at him, 'I don't know if you are really capable of succeeding in your job. I think you will not be able to avoid it. However, I am too long dead and too tired to care as much as I did. The principal reason I am helping you now is that I couldn't bear the thought of you and your modern friends slouching about up here. Understand?'

'Yeah, thanks a bundle.'

'Oh, and Zaphod?'

'Er, yeah?'

'If you ever find you need help again, you know, if you're in trouble, need a hand out of a tight corner . . .'

'Yeah?'

'Please don't hesitate to get lost.'

Within the space of one second, a bolt of light flashed from the wizened old ghost's hands to the computer, the ghost vanished, the bridge filled with billowing smoke and the *Heart of Gold* leapt an unknown distance through the dimensions of time and space.

4

Ten light-years away, Gag Halfrunt jacked up his smile by several notches. As he watched the picture on his vision screen, relayed across the sub-etha from the bridge of the Vogon ship, he saw the final shreds of the *Heart of Gold*'s force-shield ripped away, and the ship itself vanish in a puff of smoke.

Good, he thought.

The end of the last stray survivors of the demolition he had ordered on the planet Earth, he thought.

The final end of this dangerous (to the psychiatric profession) and subversive (also to the psychiatric profession) experiment to find the Question to the Ultimate Question of Life, the Universe and Everything, he thought.

There would be some celebration with his fellows tonight, and in the morning they would meet again their unhappy, bewildered and highly profitable patients, secure in the knowledge that the Meaning of Life would not now be, once and for all, well and truly sorted out, he thought.

'Family's always embarrassing, isn't it?' said Ford to Zaphod as the smoke began to clear.

He paused, he looked about.

'Where's Zaphod?' he said.

Arthur and Trillian looked about blankly. They were pale and shaken and didn't know where Zaphod was.

'Marvin?' said Ford. 'Where's Zaphod?'

'Where's Marvin?'

The robot's corner was empty.

The ship was utterly silent. It lay in thick black space. Occasionally it rocked and swayed. Every instrument was dead, every vision screen was dead. They consulted the computer. It said:

'I regret I have been temporarily closed to all communication. Meanwhile, here is some light music.'

They turned off the light music.

They searched every corner of the ship in increasing bewilderment and alarm. Everywhere was dead and silent. Nowhere was there any trace of Zaphod or of Marvin.

One of the last areas they checked was the small bay in which the Nutri-Matic machine was located.

On the delivery plate of the Nutri-Matic Drinks Synthesizer was a small tray, on which sat three bone china cups and saucers, a bone china jug of milk, a silver teapot full of the best tea Arthur had ever tasted, and a small printed note saying 'Wait'.

5

Ursa Minor Beta is, some say, one of the most appalling places in the known Universe.

Although it is excruciatingly rich, horrifyingly sunny and more full of wonderfully exciting people than a pomegranate is of pips, it can hardly be insignificant that when a recent edition of *Playbeing* magazine headlined an article with the words 'When you are tired of Ursa Minor Beta you are tired of life', the suicide rate there quadrupled overnight.

Not that there are any nights on Ursa Minor Beta.

It is a west-zone planet which by an inexplicable and somewhat suspicious freak of topography consists almost entirely of sub-tropical coastline. By an equally suspicious freak of temporal relastatics, it is nearly always Saturday afternoon just before the beach bars close.

No adequate explanation for this has been forthcoming from the dominant lifeforms on Ursa Minor Beta, who spend most of their time attempting to achieve spiritual enlightenment by running round swimming pools, and inviting Investigation Officials from the Galactic Geo-Temporal Control Board to 'have a nice diurnal anomaly'.

There is only one city on Ursa Minor Beta, and that is only called a city because the swimming pools are slightly thicker on the ground there than elsewhere.

If you approach Light City by air – and there is no other way of approaching it, no roads, no port facilities – if you don't fly they don't want to see you in Light City – you will see why it has this name. Here the sun shines brightest of all, glittering on the swimming pools, shimmering on the white, palm-lined boulevards, glistening on the healthy bronzed specks moving up and down them, gleaming off the villas, and hazy airpads, the beach bars and so on.

Most particularly it shines on a building, a tall, beautiful building consisting of two thirty-storey white towers connected by a bridge halfway up their length.

The building is the home of a book, and was built here on the proceeds of an extraordinary copyright lawsuit fought between the book's editors and a breakfast cereal company.

The book is a guide book, a travel book.

It is one of the most remarkable, certainly the most successful, books ever to come out of the great publishing corporations of Ursa Minor – more popular than *Life Begins at Five Hundred and Fifty*, better selling than *The Big Bang Theory – A Personal View* by Eccentrica Gallumbits (the triple-breasted whore of Eroticon Six) and more controversial than Oolon Colluphid's latest blockbusting title *Everything You Never Wanted To Know About Sex But Have Been Forced To Find Out*.

(And in many of the more relaxed civilizations on the Outer Eastern Rim of the Galaxy, it has long supplanted the great *Encyclopaedia Galactica* as the standard repository of all knowledge and wisdom, for though it has many omissions and contains much that is apocryphal, or at least wildly inaccurate, it scores over the older, more pedestrian work in two important respects. First, it is slightly cheaper, and secondly it has the words DON'T PANIC printed in large friendly letters on its cover.)

It is of course that invaluable companion for all those who want to see the marvels of the known Universe for less than thirty Altairian dollars a day – *The Hitchhiker's Guide to the Galaxy*.

If you stood with your back to the main entrance lobby of the *Guide* offices (assuming you had landed by now and freshened up with a quick dip and shower) and then walked east, you would pass along the leafy shade of Life Boulevard, be amazed by the pale golden colour of the beaches stretching away to your left, astounded by the mind-surfers floating carelessly along two feet above the waves as if this was nothing special, surprised and eventually slightly irritated by the giant palm trees that hum tuneless nothings throughout the daylight hours, in other words continuously.

If you then walked to the end of Life Boulevard you would enter the Lalamatine district of shops, bolonut trees and pavement cafés where the UM-Betans come to relax after a hard afternoon's relaxation on the beach.

The Lalamatine district is one of those very few areas which doesn't enjoy a perpetual Saturday afternoon – it enjoys instead the cool of a perpetual early Saturday evening. Behind it lie the nightclubs.

If, on this particular day, afternoon, stretch of eveningtime – call it what you will – you had approached the second pavement café on the right you would have seen the usual crowd of UM-Betans chatting, drinking, looking very relaxed, and casually glancing at each other's watches to see how expensive they were.

You would also have seen a couple of rather dishevelled looking hitchhikers from Algol who had recently arrived on an Arcturan megafreighter abroad which they had been roughing it for a few days. They were angry and bewildered to discover that here, within sight of the *Hitchhiker's Guide* building itself, a simple glass of fruit juice cost the equivalent of over sixty Altairian dollars.

'Sell out,' one of them said, bitterly.

If at that moment you had then looked at the next table but one you would have seen Zaphod Beeblebrox sitting and looking very startled and confused.

The reason for his confusion was that five seconds earlier he had been sitting on the bridge of the starship *Heart of Gold*.

'Absolute sell out,' said the voice again.

Zaphod looked nervously out of the corners of his eyes at the two dishevelled hitchhikers at the next table. Where the hell was he? How had he got there? Where was his ship? His hand felt the arm of the chair on which he was sitting, and then the table in front of him. They seemed solid enough. He sat very still.

'How can they sit and write a guide for hitchhikers in a place like this?' continued the voice. 'I mean look at it. Look at it!'

Zaphod was looking at it. Nice place, he thought. But where? And why?

He fished in his pocket for his two pairs of sunglasses. In the same pocket he felt a hard smooth, unidentified lump of very heavy metal. He pulled it out and looked at it. He blinked at it in surprise. Where had he got that? He returned it to his pocket and put on the sunglasses, annoyed to discover that the metal object had scratched one of the lenses. Nevertheless, he felt much more comfortable with them on. They were a double pair of Joo Janta 200 Super-Chromatic Peril-Sensitive Sunglasses, which had been specially designed to help people develop a relaxed attitude to danger. At the first hint of trouble they turn totally black and thus prevent you from seeing anything that might alarm you.

Apart from the scratch the lenses were clear. He relaxed, but only a little bit.

The angry hitchhiker continued to glare at his monstrously expensive fruit juice.

'Worst thing that ever happened to the *Guide*, moving to Ursa Minor Beta,' he grumbled, 'they've all gone soft. You know, I've even heard that they've created a whole electronically synthesized Universe in one of their offices so they can go and research stories during the day and still go to parties in the evening. Not that day and evening mean much in this place.'

Ursa Minor Beta, thought Zaphod. At least he knew where he was now. He assumed that this must be his great-grandfather's doing, but why?

Much to his annoyance, a thought popped into his mind. It was very clear and very distinct, and he had now come to recognize these thoughts for what they were. His instinct was to resist them. They were the preordained promptings from the dark and locked off parts of his mind.

He sat still and ignored the thought furiously. It nagged at him. He ignored it. It nagged at him. He ignored it. It nagged at him. He gave in to it.

What the hell, he thought, go with the flow. He was too tired, confused and hungry to resist. He didn't even know what the thought meant.

6

'Hello? Yes? Megadodo Publications, home of *The Hitchhiker's Guide to the Galaxy*, the most totally remarkable book in the whole of the known Universe, can I help you?' said the large pink-winged insect into one of the seventy phones lined up along the vast chrome expanse of the reception desk in the foyer of the *Hitchhiker's Guide to the Galaxy* offices. It fluttered its wings and rolled its eyes. It glared at all the grubby people cluttering up the foyer, soiling the carpets and leaving dirty handmarks on the upholstery. It adored working for *The Hitchhiker's Guide to the Galaxy*, it just wished there was some way of keeping all the hitchhikers away. Weren't they meant to be hanging around dirty spaceports or something? It was certain that it had read something somewhere in the book about the importance of hanging round dirty spaceports. Unfortunately most of them seemed to come and hang around in this nice clean shiny foyer immediately after hanging around in extremely dirty space ports. And all they ever did was complain. It shivered its wings.

'What?' it said into the phone. 'Yes, I passed on your message to Mr Zarniwoop, but I'm afraid he's too cool to see you right now. He's on an intergalactic cruise.'

It waved a petulant tentacle at one of the grubby people who was angrily trying to engage its attention. The petulant tentacle directed the angry person to look at the notice on the wall to its left and not to interrupt an important phone call.

'Yes,' said the insect, 'he is in his office, but he's on an intergalactic cruise. Thank you so much for calling.' It slammed down the phone.

'Read the notice,' it said to the angry man who was trying to complain about one of the more ludicrous and dangerous pieces of misinformation contained in the book.

The Hitchhiker's Guide to the Galaxy is an indispensable companion to all those who are keen to make sense of life in an infinitely complex and confusing Universe, for though it cannot hope to be useful or informative on all matters, it does at least make the reassuring claim, that where it is inaccurate it is at least *definitively* inaccurate. In cases of major discrepancy it's always reality that's got it wrong.

This was the gist of the notice. It said, 'The *Guide* is definitive. Reality is frequently inaccurate.'

This has led to some interesting consequences. For instance, when the Editors of the *Guide* were sued by the families of those who had died as a result of taking the entry on the planet Traal literally (it said 'Ravenous Bugblatter Beasts often make a very good meal for visiting tourists' instead of 'Ravenous Bugblatter Beasts often make a very good meal *of* visiting tourists') they claimed that the first version of the sentence was the more aesthetically pleasing, summoned a qualified poet to testify under oath that beauty was truth, truth beauty and hoped thereby to prove that the guilty party in this case was Life itself for failing to be either beautiful or true. The judges concurred, and in a moving speech held that Life itself was in contempt of court, and duly confiscated it from all those there present before going off to enjoy a pleasant evening's ultragolf.

Zaphod Beeblebrox entered the foyer. He strode up to the Insect receptionist.

'OK,' he said, 'where's Zarniwoop? Get me Zarniwoop.'

'Excuse me, sir?' said the insect icily. It did not care to be addressed in this manner.

'Zarniwoop. Get him, right? Get him now.'

'Well, sir,' snapped the fragile little creature, 'if you could be a little cool about it . . .'

'Look,' said Zaphod, 'I'm up to here with cool, OK? I am so amazingly cool you could keep a side of meat in me for a month. I am so hip I have difficulty seeing over my pelvis. Now will you move before I blow it?'

'Well, if you'd let me explain, *sir*,' said the insect tapping the most petulant of all the tentacles at its disposal, 'I'm afraid that isn't possible right now as Mr Zarniwoop is on an intergalactic cruise.'

Hell, thought Zaphod.

'When's he going to be back?' he said.

'Back, sir? He's in his office.'

Zaphod paused whilst he tried to sort this particular thought out in his mind. He didn't succeed.

'This cat's on an intergalactic cruise . . . in his *office*?' He leaned forward and gripped the tapping tentacle.

'Listen, three eyes,' he said, 'don't you try to outweird me, I get stranger things than you free with my breakfast cereal.'

'Well, just who do you think you are, honey,' flounced the insect quivering its wings in rage. 'Zaphod Beeblebrox or something?'

'Count the heads,' said Zaphod in a low rasp.

The insect blinked at him. It blinked at him again.

'You *are* Zaphod Beeblebrox?' it squeaked.

'Yeah,' said Zaphod, 'but don't shout it out or they'll all want one.'

'*The* Zaphod Beeblebrox?'

'No, just a Zaphod Beeblebrox, didn't you hear I come in six-packs?'

The insect rattled its tentacles together in agitation.

'But sir,' it squealed, 'I just heard on the sub-etha radio report. It said you were dead . . .'

'Yeah, that's right,' said Zaphod, 'I just haven't stopped moving yet. Now. Where do I find Zarniwoop?'

'Well sir, his office is on the fifteenth floor, but . . .'

'But he's on an intergalactic cruise, yeah, yeah, how do I get to him?'

'The newly installed Sirius Cybernetics Corporation Happy-Vertical People Transporters are in the far corner sir. But, sir . . .'

Zaphod was turning to go. He turned back.

'Yeah?' he said.

'Can I ask you why you want to see Mr Zarniwoop?'

'Yeah,' said Zaphod, who was unclear on this point himself. 'I told myself I had to.'

'Come again, sir?'

Zaphod leaned forward, conspiratorially.

'I just materialized out of thin air in one of your cafés,' he said, 'as a result of an argument with the ghost of my great-grandfather. No sooner had I got there than my former self, the one that operated on my brain, popped into my head and said, "Go see Zarniwoop." I have never heard of the cat. That is all I know. That and the fact that I've got to find the man who rules the Universe.'

He winked.

'Mr Beeblebrox, sir,' said the insect in awed wonder, 'you're so weird you should be in movies.'

'Yeah,' said Zaphod patting the thing on a glittering pink wing, 'and you, baby, should be in real life.'

The insect paused for a moment to recover from its

agitation and then reached out a tentacle to answer a ringing phone.

A metal hand restrained it.

'Excuse me,' said the owner of the metal hand in a voice that would have made an insect of a more sentimental disposition collapse in tears.

This was not such an insect, and it couldn't stand robots.

'Yes, *sir*,' it snapped, 'can I help you?'

'I doubt it,' said Marvin.

'Well in that case, if you'll just excuse me . . .' Six of the phones were now ringing. A million things awaited the insect's attention.

'No one can help me,' intoned Marvin.

'Yes, sir, well . . .'

'Not that anyone's tried, of course.' The restraining metal hand fell limply by Marvin's side. His head hung forward very slightly.

'Is that so,' the insect said tartly.

'Hardly worth anyone's while to help a menial robot, is it?'

'I'm sorry, sir, if . . .'

'I mean where's the percentage in being kind or helpful to a robot if it doesn't have any gratitude circuits?'

'And you don't have any?' said the insect, who didn't seem to be able to drag itself out of this conversation.

'I've never had occasion to find out,' Marvin informed it.

'Listen, you miserable heap of maladjusted metal . . .'

'Aren't you going to ask me what I want?'

The insect paused. Its long thin tongue darted out and licked its eyes and darted back again.

'Is it *worth* it?' it asked.

'Is anything?' said Marvin immediately.

'What . . . do . . . you . . . want?'

'I'm looking for someone.'

'Who?' hissed the insect.

'Zaphod Beeblebrox,' said Marvin, 'he's over there.'

The insect shook with rage. It could hardly speak.

'Then why did you ask *me*?' it screamed.

'I just wanted something to talk to,' said Marvin.

'What!'

'Pathetic, isn't it?'

With a grinding of gears Marvin turned and trundled off. He caught up with Zaphod approaching the elevators. Zaphod span round in astonishment.

'Hey . . . Marvin?' he said. 'Marvin! How did you get here?'

Marvin was forced to say something which came very hard to him.

'I don't know,' he said.

'But . . .'

'One moment I was sitting in your ship feeling very depressed, and the next moment I was standing here feeling utterly miserable. An Improbability Field, I expect.'

'Yeah,' said Zaphod, 'I expect my great-grandfather sent you along to keep me company.'

'Thanks a bundle, Grandad,' he added to himself under his breath.

'So, how are you?' he said aloud.

'Oh, fine,' said Marvin, 'if you happen to like being me which personally I don't.'

'Yeah, yeah,' said Zaphod as the elevator doors opened.

'Hello,' said the elevator sweetly, 'I am to be your elevator for this trip to the floor of your choice. I have been designed by the Sirius Cybernetics Corporation to take you, the visitor to *The Hitchhiker's Guide to the*

Galaxy, into these their offices. If you enjoy your ride, which will be swift and pleasurable, then you may care to experience some of the other elevators which have recently been installed in the offices of the Galactic tax department, Boobiloo Baby Foods and the Sirian State Mental Hospital, where many ex-Sirius Cybernetics Corporation executives will be delighted to welcome your visits, sympathy and happy tales of the outside world.'

'Yeah,' said Zaphod, stepping into it, 'what else do you do besides talk?'

'I go up,' said the elevator, 'or down.'

'Good,' said Zaphod. 'We're going up.'

'Or down,' the elevator reminded him.

'Yeah, OK, up please.'

There was a moment of silence.

'Down's very nice,' suggested the elevator hopefully.

'Oh yeah?'

'Super.'

'Good,' said Zaphod. 'Now will you take us up?'

'May I ask you,' enquired the elevator in its sweetest, most reasonable voice, 'if you've considered all the possibilities that down might offer you?'

Zaphod knocked one of his heads against the inside wall. He didn't need this, he thought to himself, this of all things he had no need of. He hadn't asked to be here. If he was asked at this moment where he would like to be he would probably have said he would like to be lying on the beach with at least fifty beautiful women and a small team of experts working out new ways they could be nice to him, which was his usual reply. To this he would probably have added something passionate on the subject of food.

One thing he didn't want to be doing was chasing after the man who ruled the Universe, who was only doing a job which he might as well keep at, because if it wasn't him it would only be someone else. Most of all he didn't want to be standing in an office block arguing with an elevator.

'Like what other possibilities?' he said wearily.

'Well,' the voice trickled on like honey on biscuits, 'there's the basement, the microfiles, the heating system . . . er . . .'

It paused.

'Nothing particularly exciting,' it admitted, 'but they are alternatives.'

'Holy Zarquon,' muttered Zaphod, 'did I *ask* for an existential elevator?' He beat his fists against the wall.

'What's the matter with the thing?' he spat.

'It doesn't want to go up,' said Marvin simply, 'I think it's afraid.'

'Afraid?' cried Zaphod. 'Of what? Heights? An elevator that's afraid of heights?'

'No,' said the elevator miserably, 'of the future . . .'

'The *future*?' exclaimed Zaphod. 'What does the wretched thing want, a pension scheme?'

At that moment a commotion broke out in the reception hall behind them. From the walls around them came the sound of suddenly active machinery.

'We can all see into the future,' whispered the elevator in what sounded like terror, 'it's part of our programming.'

Zaphod looked out of the elevator – an agitated crowd had gathered round the elevator area, pointing and shouting.

Every elevator in the building was coming down, very fast.

He ducked back in.

'Marvin,' he said, 'just get this elevator to go up, will you? We've got to get to Zarniwoop.'

'Why?' said Marvin dolefully.

'I don't know,' said Zaphod, 'but when I find him,

he'd better have a very good reason for me wanting to see him.'

Modern elevators are strange and complex entities. The ancient electric winch and 'maximum capacity eight persons' jobs bear as much relation to a Sirius Cybernetics Corporation Happy Vertical People Transporter as a packet of mixed nuts does to the entire west wing of the Sirian State Mental Hospital.

This is because they operate on the curious principle of 'defocused temporal perception'. In other words they have the capacity to see dimly into the immediate future, which enables the elevator to be on the right floor to pick you up even before you knew you wanted it, thus eliminating all the tedious chatting, relaxing, and making friends that people were previously forced to do whilst waiting for elevators.

Not unnaturally, many elevators imbued with intelligence and precognition became terribly frustrated with the mindless business of going up and down, up and down, experimented briefly with the notion of going sideways, as a sort of existential protest, demanded participation in the decision-making process and finally took to squatting in basements sulking.

An impoverished hitchhiker visiting any planets in the Sirius star system these days can pick up easy money working as a counsellor for neurotic elevators.

At the fifteenth floor the elevator doors snapped open quickly.

'Fifteenth,' said the elevator, 'and remember, I'm only doing this because I like your robot.'

Zaphod and Marvin bundled out of the elevator which instantly snapped its doors shut and dropped as fast as its mechanism would take it.

Zaphod looked around warily. The corridor was

deserted and silent and gave no clue as to where Zarniwoop might be found. All the doors that led off the corridor were closed and unmarked.

They were standing close to the bridge which led across from one tower of the building to the other. Through a large window the brilliant sun of Ursa Minor Beta threw blocks of light in which danced small specks of dust. A shadow flitted past momentarily.

'Left in the lurch by a lift,' muttered Zaphod, who was feeling at his least jaunty.

They both stood and looked in both directions.

'You know something?' said Zaphod to Marvin.

'More than you can possibly imagine.'

'I'm dead certain this building shouldn't be shaking,' Zaphod said.

It was just a light tremor through the soles of his feet – and another one. In the sunbeams the flecks of dust danced more vigorously. Another shadow flitted past.

Zaphod looked at the floor.

'Either,' he said, not very confidently, 'they've got some vibro system for toning up your muscles while you work, or . . .'

He walked across to the window and suddenly stumbled because at that moment his Joo Janta 200 Super-Chromatic Peril-Sensitive sunglasses had turned utterly black. A large shadow flitted past the window with a sharp buzz.

Zaphod ripped off his sunglasses, and as he did so the building shook with a thunderous roar. He leapt to the window.

'Or,' he said, 'this building's being bombed!'

Another roar cracked through the building.

'Who in the Galaxy would want to bomb a publishing company?' asked Zaphod, but never heard Marvin's reply because at that moment the building shook with another bomb attack. He tried to stagger back to the elevator – a pointless maneouvre, he realized, but the only one he could think of.

Suddenly, at the end of a corridor leading at right angles from this one, he caught sight of a figure as it lunged into view, a man. The man saw him.

'Beeblebrox, over here!' he shouted.

Zaphod eyed him with distrust as another bomb blast rocked the building.

'No,' called Zaphod, 'Beeblebrox over here! Who are you?'

'A friend!' shouted back the man. He ran towards Zaphod.

'Oh yeah?' said Zaphod. 'Anyone's friend in particular, or just generally well-disposed to people?'

The man raced along the corridor, the floor bucking beneath his feet like an excited blanket. He was short, stocky and weatherbeaten and his clothes looked as if they'd been twice round the Galaxy and back with him in them.

'Do you know,' Zaphod shouted in his ear when he arrived, 'your building's being bombed?'

The man indicated his awareness.

It suddenly stopped being light. Glancing round at the window to see why, Zaphod gaped as a huge slug-like, gun-metal-green spacecraft crept through the air past the building. Two more followed it.

'The government you deserted is out to get you, Zaphod,' hissed the man, 'they've sent a squadron of Frogstar Fighters.'

'Frogstar Fighters!' muttered Zaphod. 'Zarquon!'

'You get the picture?'

'What are Frogstar Fighters?' Zaphod was sure he'd heard someone talk about them when he was President, but he never paid much attention to official matters.

The man was pulling him back through a door. He went with him. With a searing whine a small black spider-like object shot through the air and disappeared down the corridor.

'What was that?' hissed Zaphod.

'Frogstar Scout robot class A out looking for you,' said the man.

'Hey yeah?'

'Get down!'

From the opposite direction came a larger black spider-like object. It zapped past them.

'And that was . . .?'

'A Frogstar Scout robot class B out looking for you.'

'And that?' said Zaphod, as a third one seared through the air.

'A Frogstar Scout robot class C out looking for you.'

'Hey,' chuckled Zaphod to himself, 'pretty stupid robots, eh?'

From over the bridge came a massive rumbling hum. A gigantic black shape was moving over it from the opposite tower, the size and shape of a tank.

'Holy photon, what's that?' breathed Zaphod.

'A tank,' said the man, 'Frogstar Scout robot class D come to get you.'

'Should we leave?'

'I think we should.'

'Marvin!' called Zaphod.

'What do you want?'

Marvin rose from a pile of rubble further down the corridor and looked at them.

'You see that robot coming towards us?'

Marvin looked at the gigantic black shape edging forward towards them over the bridge. He looked down at his own small metal body. He looked back up at the tank.

'I suppose you want me to stop it,' he said.

'Yeah.'

'Whilst you save your skins.'

'Yeah,' said Zaphod, 'get in there!'

'Just so long,' said Marvin, 'as I know where I stand.'

The man tugged at Zaphod's arm, and Zaphod followed him off down the corridor.

A point occurred to him about this.

'Where are we going?' he said.

'Zarniwoop's office.'

'Is this any time to keep an appointment?'

'Come on.'

7

Marvin stood at the end of the bridge corridor. He was not in fact a particularly small robot. His silver body gleamed in the dusty sunbeams and shook with the continual barrage which the building was still undergoing.

He did, however, look pitifully small as the gigantic black tank rolled to a halt in front of him. The tank examined him with a probe. The probe withdrew.

Marvin stood there.

'Out of my way, little robot,' growled the tank.

'I'm afraid,' said Marvin, 'that I've been left here to stop you.'

The probe extended again for a quick recheck. It withdrew again.

'You? Stop me?' roared the tank. 'Go on!'

'No, really I have,' said Marvin simply.

'What are you armed with?' roared the tank in disbelief.

'Guess,' said Marvin.

The tank's engines rumbled, its gears ground. Molecule-sized electronic relays deep in its micro-brain flipped backwards and forwards in consternation.

'Guess?' said the tank.

Zaphod and the as yet unnamed man lurched up one corridor, down a second and along a third. The building continued to rock and judder and this puzzled Zaphod. If they wanted to blow the building up, why was it taking so long?

With difficulty they reached one of a number of totally anonymous unmarked doors and heaved at it. With a sudden jolt it opened and they fell inside.

All this way, thought Zaphod, all this trouble, all this not-lying-on-the-beach-having-a-wonderful-time, and for what? A single chair, a single desk and a single dirty ashtray in an undecorated office. The desk, apart from a bit of dancing dust and single, revolutionary new form of paper clip, was empty.

'Where,' said Zaphod, 'is Zarniwoop?' feeling that his already tenuous grasp of the point of this whole exercise was beginning to slip.

'He's on an intergalactic cruise,' said the man.

Zaphod tried to size the man up. Earnest type, he thought, not a barrel of laughs. He probably apportioned a fair whack of his time to running up and down heaving corridors, breaking down doors and making cryptic remarks in empty offices.

'Let me introduce myself,' the man said. 'My name is Roosta, and this is my towel.'

'Hello, Roosta,' said Zaphod.

'Hello, towel,' he added as Roosta held out to him a rather nasty old flowery towel. Not knowing what to do with it, he shook it by the corner.

Outside the window, one of the huge slug-like, gunmetal-green spaceships growled past.

*

'Yes, go on,' said Marvin to the huge battle machine, 'you'll never guess.'

'Errrmmm . . .' said the machine, vibrating with unaccustomed thought, 'laser beams?'

Marvin shook his head solemnly.

'No,' muttered the machine in its deep guttural rumble, 'Too obvious. Anti-matter ray?' it hazarded.

'Far too obvious,' admonished Marvin.

'Yes,' grumbled the machine, somewhat abashed. 'Er . . . how about an electron ram?'

This was new to Marvin.

'What's that?' he said.

'One of these,' said the machine with enthusiasm.

From its turret emerged a sharp prong which spat a single lethal blaze of light. Behind Marvin a wall roared and collapsed as a heap of dust. The dust billowed briefly, then settled.

'No,' said Marvin, 'not one of those.'

'Good though, isn't it?'

'Very good,' agreed Marvin.

'I know,' said the Frogstar battle machine, after another moment's consideration, 'you must have one of those new Xanthic Re-Structron Destabilized Zenon Emitters!'

'Nice, aren't they?' said Marvin.

'That's what you've got?' said the machine in considerable awe.

'No,' said Marvin.

'Oh,' said the machine, disappointed, 'then it must be . . .'

'You're thinking along the wrong lines,' said Marvin. 'You're failing to take into account something fairly basic in the relationship between men and robots.'

'Er, I know,' said the battle machine, 'is it . . .' it tailed off into thought again.

'Just think,' urged Marvin, 'they left me, an ordinary,

menial robot, to stop you, a gigantic heavy-duty battle machine, whilst they ran off to save themselves. What do you think they would leave me with?'

'Oooh er,' muttered the machine in alarm, 'something pretty damn devastating, I should expect.'

'Expect!' said Marvin, 'oh yes, expect. I'll tell you what they gave me to protect myself with shall I?'

'Yes, all right,' said the battle machine, bracing itself.

'Nothing,' said Marvin.

There was a dangerous pause.

'*Nothing?*' roared the battle machine.

'Nothing at all,' intoned Marvin dismally, 'not an electronic sausage.'

The machine heaved about with fury.

'Well, doesn't that just take the biscuit!' it roared. 'Nothing, eh? Just don't think, do they?'

'And me,' said Marvin in a soft low voice, 'with this terrible pain in all the diodes down my left side.'

'Makes you spit, doesn't it?'

'Yes,' agreed Marvin with feeling.

'Hell that makes me angry,' bellowed the machine, 'think I'll smash that wall down!'

The electron ram stabbed out another searing blaze of light and took out the wall next to the machine.

'How do you think I feel?' said Marvin bitterly.

'Just ran off and left you, did they?' the machine thundered.

'Yes,' said Marvin.

'I think I'll shoot down their bloody ceiling as well!' raged the tank.

It took out the ceiling of the bridge.

'That's very impressive,' murmured Marvin.

'You ain't seen nothing yet,' promised the machine, 'I can take out this floor too, no trouble!'

It took out the floor too.

'Hell's bells!' the machine roared as it plummeted fifteen storeys and smashed itself to bits on the ground below.

'What a depressingly stupid machine,' said Marvin and trudged away.

8

'So, do we just sit here, or what?' said Zaphod angrily. 'What do these guys out here want?'

'You, Beeblebrox,' said Roosta. 'They're going to take you to the Frogstar – the most totally evil world in the Galaxy.'

'Oh yeah?' said Zaphod. 'They'll have to come and get me first.'

'They have come and got you,' said Roosta, 'look out of the window.'

Zaphod looked, and gaped.

'The ground's going away!' he gasped. 'Where are they taking the ground?'

'They're taking the building,' said Roosta, 'we're airborne.'

Clouds streaked past the office window.

Out in the open air again Zaphod could see the ring of dark-green Frogstar Fighters round the uprooted tower of the building. A network of force beams radiated in from them and held the tower in a firm grip.

Zaphod shook his head in perplexity.

'What have I done to deserve this?' he said. 'I walk into a building, they take it away.'

'It's not what you've done they're worried about,' said Roosta, 'it's what you're going to do.'

'Well, don't I get a say in that?'

'You did, years ago. You'd better hold on, we're in for a fast and bumpy journey.'

'If I ever meet myself,' said Zaphod, 'I'll hit myself so hard I won't know what's hit me.'

Marvin trudged in through the door, looked at Zaphod accusingly, slumped in a corner and switched himself off.

On the bridge of the *Heart of Gold*, all was silent. Arthur stared at the rack in front of him and thought. He caught Trillian's eyes as she looked at him enquiringly. He looked back at the rack.

Finally he saw it.

He picked up five small plastic squares and laid them on the board that lay just in front of the rack.

The five squares had on them the five letters E, X, Q, U and I. He laid them next to the letters S, I, T, E.

'Exquisite,' he said, 'on a triple word score. Scores rather a lot, I'm afraid.'

The ship bumped and scattered some of the letters for the *n* th time.

Trillian sighed and started to sort them out again.

Up and down the silent corridors echoed Ford Prefect's feet as he stalked the ship thumping dead instruments.

Why did the ship keep shaking? he thought.

Why did it rock and sway?

Why could he not find out where they were?

Where, basically, were they?

The left-hand tower of the *Hitchhiker's Guide to the Galaxy* offices streaked through interstellar space at a speed never equalled either before or since by any other office block in the Universe.

In a room halfway up it, Zaphod Beeblebrox strode angrily.

Roosta sat on the edge of the desk doing some routine towel maintenance.

'Hey, where did you say this building was flying to?' demanded Zaphod.

'The Frogstar,' said Roosta, 'the most totally evil place in the Universe.'

'Do they have food there?' said Zaphod.

'Food? You're going to the Frogstar and you're worried about whether they got food?'

'Without food I may not make it to the Frogstar.'

Out of the window, they could see nothing but the flickering light of the force beams, and vague green streaks which were presumably the distorted shapes of the Frogstar Fighters. At this speed, space itself was invisible, and indeed unreal.

'Here, suck this,' said Roosta, offering Zaphod his towel.

Zaphod stared at him as if he expected a cuckoo to leap out of his forehead on a small spring.

'It's soaked in nutrients,' explained Roosta.

'What are you, a messy eater or something?' said Zaphod.

'The yellow stripes are high in protein, the green ones have vitamin B and C complexes, the little pink flowers contain wheatgerm extract.'

Zaphod took and looked at it in amazement.

'What are the brown stains?' he asked.

'Bar-B-Q sauce,' said Roosta, 'for when I get sick of wheatgerm.'

Zaphod sniffed it doubtfully.

Even more doubtfully, he sucked a corner. He spat it out again.

'Ugh,' he stated.

'Yes,' said Roosta, 'when I've had to suck that end I usually need to suck the other end a bit too.'

'Why,' asked Zaphod suspiciously, 'what's in that?'

'Anti-depressants,' said Roosta.

'I've gone right off this towel, you know,' said Zaphod handing it back.

Roosta took it back from him, swung himself off the desk walked round it, sat in the chair and put his feet up.

'Beeblebrox,' he said, sticking his hands behind his head, 'have you any idea what's going to happen to you on the Frogstar?'

'They're going to feed me?' hazarded Zaphod hopefully.

'They're going to feed you,' said Roosta, 'into the Total Perspective Vortex!'

Zaphod had never heard of this. He believed that he had heard of all the fun things in the Galaxy, so he assumed that the Total Perspective Vortex was not fun. He asked Roosta what it was.

'Only,' said Roosta, 'the most savage psychic torture a sentient being can undergo.'

Zaphod nodded a resigned nod.

'So,' he said, 'no food, huh?'

'Listen!' said Roosta urgently. 'You can kill a man, destroy his body, break his spirit, but only the Total Perspective Vortex can annihilate a man's soul! The treatment lasts seconds, but the effects last the rest of your life!'

'You ever had a Pan Galactic Gargle Blaster?' asked Zaphod sharply.

'This is worse.'

'Phreeow!' admitted Zaphod, much impressed.

'Any idea why these guys might want to do this to me?' he added a moment later.

'They believe it will be the best way of destroying you for ever. They know what you're after.'

'Could they drop me a note and let me know as well?'

'You know,' said Roosta, 'you know, Beeblebrox. You want to meet the man who rules the Universe.'

'Can he cook?' said Zaphod. On reflection he added: 'I doubt if he can. If he could cook a good meal he wouldn't worry about the rest of the Universe. I want to meet a cook.'

Roosta sighed heavily.

'What are you doing here, anyway?' demanded Zaphod. 'What's all this got to do with you?'

'I'm just one of those who planned this thing, along with Zarniwoop, along with Yooden Vranx, along with your great-grandfather, along with you, Beeblebrox.'

'Me?'

'Yes, you. I was told you had changed, I didn't realize how much.'

'But . . .'

'I am here to do one job. I will do it before I leave you.'

'What job, man, what are you talking about?'

'I will do it before I leave you.'

Roosta lapsed into an impenetrable silence.

Zaphod was terribly glad.

9

The air around the second planet of the Frogstar system was stale and unwholesome.

The dank winds that swept continually over its surface swept over salt flats, dried-up marshland, tangled and rotting vegetation and the crumbling remains of ruined cities. No life moved across its surface. The ground, like that of many planets in this part of the Galaxy, had long been deserted.

The howl of the wind was desolate enough as it gusted through the old decaying houses of the cities; it was more desolate as it whipped about the bottoms of the tall black towers that swayed uneasily here and there about the surface of this world. At the top of these towers lived colonies of large, scraggy, evil-smelling birds, the sole survivors of the civilization that once lived here.

The howl of the wind was at its most desolate, however, when it passed over a pimple of a place set in the middle of a wide grey plain on the outskirts of the largest of the abandoned cities.

This pimple of a place was the thing that had earned this world the reputation of being the most totally evil place in the Galaxy. From without it was simply a steel dome about thirty feet across. From within it was something more monstrous than the mind can comprehend.

About a hundred yards or so away, and separated from it by a pockmarked and blasted stretch of the most barren land imaginable was what would probably have to be described as a landing pad of sorts. That is to say that scattered over a largish area were the ungainly hulks of two or three dozen crash-landed buildings.

Flitting over and around these buildings was a mind, a mind that was waiting for something.

The mind directed its attention into the air, and before very long a distant speck appeared, surrounded by a ring of smaller specks.

The larger speck was the left-hand tower of the *Hitchhiker's Guide to the Galaxy* office building, descending through the stratosphere of Frogstar World B.

As it descended, Roosta suddenly broke the long

uncomfortable silence that had grown up between the two men.

He stood up and gathered his towel into a bag. He said: 'Beeblebrox, I will now do the job I was sent here to do.'

Zaphod looked up at him from where he was sitting in a corner sharing unspoken thoughts with Marvin.

'Yeah?' he said.

'The building will shortly be landing. When you leave the building, do not go out of the door,' said Roosta, 'go out of the window.'

'Good luck,' he added, and walked out of the door, disappearing from Zaphod's life as mysteriously as he had entered it.

Zaphod leapt up and tried the door, but Roosta had already locked it. He shrugged and returned to the corner.

Two minutes later, the building crashlanded amongst the other wreckage. Its escort of Frogstar Fighters deactivated their force beams and soared off into the air again, bound for Frogstar World A, an altogether more congenial spot. They never landed on Frogstar World B. No one did. No one ever walked on its surface other than the intended victims of the Total Perspective Vortex.

Zaphod was badly shaken by the crash. He lay for a while in the silent dusty rubble to which most of the room had been reduced. He felt that he was at the lowest ebb he had ever reached in his life. He felt bewildered, he felt lonely, he felt unloved. Eventually he felt he ought to get whatever it was over with.

He looked around the cracked and broken room. The wall had split round the door frame, and the door hung open. The window, by some miracle, was closed and unbroken. For a while he hesitated, then he thought that if his strange and recent companion had been through all that he had been through just to tell him what he had told him, then there must be a good reason for it. With Marvin's help he got the window open. Outside it, the cloud of dust aroused by the crash, and the hulks of the other buildings with which this one was surrounded, effectively prevented Zaphod from seeing anything of the world outside.

Not that this concerned him unduly. His main concern was what he saw when he looked down. Zarniwoop's office was on the fifteenth floor. The building had landed at a tilt of about forty-five degrees, but still the descent looked heart-stopping.

Eventually, stung by the continuous series of contemptuous looks that Marvin appeared to be giving him, he took a deep breath and clambered out on to the steeply inclined side of the building. Marvin followed him, and together they began to crawl slowly and painfully down the fifteen floors that separated them from the ground.

As he crawled, the dank air and dust choked his lungs, his eyes smarted and the terrifying distance down made his heads spin.

The occasional remark from Marvin of the order of, 'This is the sort of thing you lifeforms enjoy is it? I ask merely for information,' did little to improve his state of mind.

About halfway down the side of the shattered building they stopped to rest. It seemed to Zaphod as he lay there panting with fear and exhaustion that Marvin seemed a mite more cheerful than usual. Eventually he realized this wasn't so. The robot just seemed cheerful in comparison with his own mood.

A large, scraggy black bird came flapping through the slowly settling clouds of dust and, stretching down its scrawny legs, landed on an inclined window ledge a couple of yards from Zaphod. It folded its ungainly wings and teetered awkwardly on its perch.

Its wingspan must have been something life six feet, and its head and neck seemed curiously large for a bird. Its face was flat, the beak underdeveloped, and halfway along the underside of its wings the vestige of something handlike could be clearly seen.

In fact, it looked almost human.

It turned its heavy eyes on Zaphod and clicked its beak in a desultory fashion.

'Go away,' said Zaphod.

'OK,' muttered the bird morosely and flapped off into the dust again.

Zaphod watched its departure in bewilderment.

'Did that bird just talk to me?' he asked Marvin nervously. He was quite prepared to believe the alternative explanation, that he was in fact hallucinating.

'Yes,' confirmed Marvin.

'Poor souls,' said a deep, ethereal voice in Zaphod's ear.

Twisting round violently to find the source of the voice nearly caused Zaphod to fall off the building. He grabbed savagely at a protruding window fitting and cut his hand on it. He hung on, breathing heavily.

The voice had no visible source whatsoever – there was no one there. Nevertheless, it spoke again.

'A tragic history behind them, you know. A terrible blight.'

Zaphod looked wildly about. The voice was deep and quiet. In other circumstances it would even be described as soothing. There is, however, nothing soothing about being addressed by a disembodied voice out of nowhere, particularly when you are, like Zaphod Beeblebrox, not at your best and hanging from a ledge eight storeys up a crashed building.

'Hey, er . . .' he stammered.

'Shall I tell you their story?' enquired the voice quietly.

'Hey, who are you?' panted Zaphod. 'Where are you?'

'Later then, perhaps,' murmured the voice. 'I am Gargravarr. I am the Custodian of the Total Perspective Vortex.'

'Why can't I see . . .'

'You will find your progress down the building greatly facilitated,' the voice lifted, 'if you move about two yards to your left. Why don't you try it?'

Zaphod looked and saw a series of short horizontal grooves leading all the way down the side of the building. Gratefully he shifted himself across to them.

'Why don't I see you again at the bottom?' said the voice in his ear, and as it spoke it faded.

'Hey,' called out Zaphod. 'Where are you . . .'

'It'll only take you a couple of minutes . . .' said the voice very faintly.

'Marvin,' said Zaphod earnestly to the robot squatting dejectedly next to him, 'did a . . . did a voice just . . .'

'Yes,' Marvin replied tersely.

Zaphod nodded. He took out his Peril-Sensitive Sunglasses again. They were completely black, and by now quite badly scratched by the unexpected metal object in his pocket. He put them on. He would find his way down the building more comfortably if he didn't actually have to look at what he was doing.

Minutes later he clambered over the ripped and mangled foundations of the building and, once more removing his sunglasses, he dropped to the ground.

Marvin joined him a moment or so later and lay face down in the dust and rubble, from which position he seemed disinclined to move.

'Ah, there you are,' said the voice suddenly in Zaphod's ear, 'excuse me leaving you like that, it's just that I have a terrible head for heights. At least,' it added wistfully, 'I did have a terrible head for heights.'

Zaphod looked around slowly and carefully, just to see if he had missed something which might be the source of the voice. All he saw, however, was the dust, the rubble and the towering hulks of the encircling buildings.

'Hey, er, why can't I see you?' he said. 'Why aren't you here?'

'*I* am here,' said the voice slowly. 'My body wanted to come but it's a bit busy at the moment. Things to do, people to see.' After what seemed like a sort of ethereal sigh it added, 'You know how it is with bodies.'

Zaphod wasn't sure about this.

'I thought I did,' he said.

'I only hope it's gone in for a rest cure,' continued the voice, 'the way it's been living recently it must be on its last elbows.'

'Elbows?' said Zaphod. 'Don't you mean last legs?'

The voice said nothing for a while. Zaphod looked around uneasily. He didn't know if it had gone or was still there or what it was doing. Then the voice spoke again.

'So, you are to be put into the Vortex, yes?'

'Er, well,' said Zaphod with a very poor attempt at nonchalance, 'this cat's in no hurry, you know. I can just slouch about and take in a look at the local scenery, you know?'

'Have you seen the local scenery?' asked the voice of Gargravarr.

'Er, no.'

Zaphod clambered over the rubble, and rounded the corner of one of the wrecked buildings that was obscuring his view.

He looked out at the landscape of Frogstar World B.

'Ah, OK,' he said, 'I'll just sort of slouch about, then.'

'No,' said Gargravarr, 'the Vortex is ready for you now. You must come. Follow me.'

'Er, yeah?' said Zaphod. 'And how am I meant to do that?'

'I'll hum for you,' said Gargravarr. 'Follow the humming.'

A soft keening sound drifted through the air, a pale, sad sound that seemed to be without any kind of focus. It was only by listening very carefully that Zaphod was able to detect the direction from which it was coming. Slowly, dazedly, he stumbled off in its wake. What else was there to do?

10

The Universe, as has been observed before, is an unsettlingly big place, a fact which for the sake of a quiet life most people tend to ignore.

Many would happily move to somewhere rather smaller of their own devising, and this is what most beings in fact do.

For instance, in one corner of the Eastern Galactic Arm lies the large forest planet Oglaroon, the entire 'intelligent' population of which lives permanently in one fairly small and crowded nut tree. In which tree they are born, live, fall in love, carve tiny speculative articles in the bark on the meaning of life, the futility of death and the importance of birth control, fight a few extremely minor wars, and eventually die strapped to the underside of some of the less accessible outer branches.

In fact the only Oglaroonians who ever leave their

tree are those who are hurled out of it for the heinous crime of wondering whether any of the other trees might be capable of supporting life at all, or indeed whether the other trees are anything other than illusions brought on by eating too many Oglanuts.

Exotic though this behaviour may seem, there is no life form in the galaxy which is not in some way guilty of the same thing, which is why the Total Perspective Vortex is as horrific as it is.

For when you are put into the Vortex you are given just one momentary glimpse of the entire unimaginable infinity of creation, and somewhere in it a tiny little market, a microscopic dot on a microscopic dot, which says 'You are here.'

The grey plain stretched before Zaphod, a ruined, shattered plain. The wind whipped wildly over it.

Visible in the middle was the steel pimple of the dome. This, gathered Zaphod, was where he was going. This was the Total Perspective Vortex.

As he stood and gazed bleakly at it, a sudden inhuman wail of terror emanated from it as of a man having his soul burnt from his body. It screamed above the wind and died away.

Zaphod stared with fear and his blood seemed to turn to liquid helium.

'Hey, what was that?' he muttered voicelessly.

'A recording,' said Gargravarr, 'of the last man who was put in the Vortex. It is always played to the next victim. A sort of prelude.'

'Hey, it really sounds bad ...' stammered Zaphod, 'couldn't we maybe slope off to a party or something for a while, think it over?'

'For all I know,' said Gargravarr's ethereal voice, 'I'm probably at one. My body that is. It goes to a lot of parties without me. Says I only get in the way. Hey ho.'

'What is all this with your body?' said Zaphod, anxious to delay whatever it was that was going to happen to him.

'Well, it's . . . it's busy, you know,' said Gargravarr hesitantly.

'You mean it's got a mind of its own?' said Zaphod.

There was a long and slightly chilly pause before Gargravarr spoke again.

'I have to say,' he replied eventually, 'that I find that remark in rather poor taste.'

Zaphod muttered a bewildered and embarrassed apology.

'No matter,' said Gargravarr, 'you weren't to know.'

The voice fluttered unhappily.

'The truth is,' it continued in tones which suggested he was trying very hard to keep it under control, 'the truth is that we are currently undergoing a period of legal trial separation. I suspect it will end in divorce.'

The voice was still again, leaving Zaphod with no idea of what to say. He mumbled uncertainly.

'I think we were probably not very well suited,' said Gargravarr again at length, 'we never seemed to be happy doing the same things. We always had the greatest arguments over sex and fishing. Eventually we tried to combine the two, but that only led to disaster, as you can probably imagine. And now my body refuses to let me in. It won't even see me . . .'

He paused again, tragically. The wind whipped across the plain.

'It says I only inhibit it. I pointed out that in fact I was meant to inhabit it, and it said that that was exactly the sort of smart-alec remark that got right up a body's left nostril, and so we left it. It will probably get custody of my forename.'

'Oh . . .?' said Zaphod faintly. 'And what's that?'

'Pizpot,' said the voice. 'My name is Pizpot Gargravarr. Says it all really, doesn't it?'

'Errr . . .' said Zaphod sympathetically.

'And that is why I, as a disembodied mind, have this job, Custodian of the Total Perspective Vortex. No one will ever walk on the ground of this planet. Except the victims of the Vortex – they don't really count I'm afraid.'

'Ah . . .'

'I'll tell you the story. Would you like to hear it?'

'Er . . .'

'Many years ago this was a thriving, happy planet – people, cities, shops, a normal world. Except that on the high streets of these cities there were slightly more shoe shops than one might have thought necessary. And slowly, insidiously, the numbers of these shoe shops were increasing. It's a well-known economic phenomenon but tragic to see it in operation, for the more shoe shops there were, the more shoes they had to make and the worse and more unwearable they became. And the worse they were to wear, the more people had to buy to keep themselves shod, and the more the shops proliferated, until the whole economy of the place passed what I believe is termed the Shoe Event Horizon, and it became no longer economically possible to build anything other than shoe shops. Result – collapse, ruin and famine. Most of the population died out. Those few who had the right kind of genetic instability mutated into birds – you've seen one of them – who cursed their feet, cursed the ground, and vowed that none should walk on it again. Unhappy lot. Come, I must take you to the Vortex.'

Zaphod shook his head in bemusement and stumbled forward across the plain.

'And you,' he said, 'you come from this hellhole pit, do you?'

'No no,' said Gargravarr, taken aback, 'I come from the Frogstar World C. Beautiful place. Wonderful fishing. I flit back there in the evenings. Though all I can do now is watch. The Total Perspective Vortex is the only thing on this planet with any function. It was built here because no one else wanted it on their doorstep.'

At that moment another dismal scream rent the air and Zaphod shuddered.

'What can do that to a guy?' he breathed.

'The Universe,' said Gargravarr simply, 'the whole infinite Universe. The infinite suns, the infinite distances between them, and yourself an invisible dot on an invisible dot, infinitely small.'

'Hey, I'm Zaphod Beeblebrox, man, you know,' muttered Zaphod trying to flap the last remnants of his ego.

Gargravarr made no reply, but merely resumed his mournful humming till they reached the tarnished steel dome in the middle of the plain.

As they reached it, a door hummed open in the side, revealing a small darkened chamber within.

'Enter,' said Gargravarr.

Zaphod started with fear.

'Hey, what, now?' he said.

'Now.'

Zaphod peered nervously inside. The chamber was very small. It was steel-lined and there was hardly space in it for more than one man.

'It . . . er . . . it doesn't look like any kind of Vortex to me,' said Zaphod.

'It isn't,' said Gargravarr, 'it's just the elevator. Enter.'

With infinite trepidation Zaphod stepped into it. He was aware of Gargravarr being in the elevator with him, though the disembodied man was not for the moment speaking.

The elevator began its descent.

'I must get myself into the right frame of mind for this,' muttered Zaphod.

'There is no right frame of mind,' said Gargravarr sternly.

'You really know how to make a guy feel inadequate.'

'I don't. The Vortex does.'

At the bottom of the shaft, the rear of the elevator opened up and Zaphod stumbled out into a smallish, functional, steel-lined chamber.

At the far side of it stood a single upright steel box, just large enough for a man to stand in.

It was that simple.

It connected to a small pile of components and instruments via a single thick wire.

'Is that it?' said Zaphod in surprise.

'That is it.'

Didn't look too bad, thought Zaphod.

'And I get in there, do I?' said Zaphod.

'You get in there,' said Gargravarr, 'and I'm afraid you must do it now.'

'OK, OK,' said Zaphod.

He opened the door of the box and stepped in.

Inside the box he waited.

After five seconds there was a click, and the entire Universe was there in the box with him.

11

The Total Perspective Vortex derives its picture of the whole Universe on the principle of extrapolated matter analyses.

To explain – since every piece of matter in the

Universe is in some way affected by every other piece of matter in the Universe, it is in theory possible to extrapolate the whole of creation – every sun, every planet, their orbits, their composition and their economic and social history from, say, one small piece of fairy cake.

The man who invented the Total Perspective Vortex did so basically in order to annoy his wife.

Trin Tragula – for that was his name – was a dreamer, a thinker, a speculative philosopher or, as his wife would have it, an idiot.

And she would nag him incessantly about the utterly inordinate amount of time he spent staring out into space, or mulling over the mechanics of safety pins, or doing spectrographic analyses of pieces of fairy cake.

'Have some sense of proportion!' she would say, sometimes as often as thirty-eight times in a single day.

And so he built the Total Perspective Vortex – just to show her.

And into one end he plugged the whole of reality as extrapolated from a piece of fairy cake, and into the other end he plugged his wife: so that when he turned it on she saw in one instant the whole infinity of creation and herself in relation to it.

To Trin Tragula's horror, the shock completely annihilated her brain; but to his satisfaction he realized that he had proved conclusively that if life is going to exist in a Universe of this size, then the one thing it cannot afford to have is a sense of proportion.

The door of the Vortex swung open.

From his disembodied mind Gargravarr watched dejectedly. He had rather liked Zaphod Beeblebrox in a strange sort of way. He was clearly a man of many qualities, even if they were mostly bad ones.

He waited for him to flop forwards out of the box, as they all did.

Instead, he stepped out.

'Hi!' he said.

'Beeblebrox . . .' gasped Gargravarr's mind in amazement.

'Could I have a drink, please?' said Zaphod.

'You . . . you . . . have been in the Vortex?' stammered Gargravarr.

'You saw me, kid.'

'And it was working?'

'Sure was.'

'And you saw the whole infinity of creation?'

'Sure. Really neat place, you know that?'

Gargravarr's mind was reeling in astonishment. Had his body been with him it would have sat down heavily with its mouth hanging open.

'And you saw yourself,' said Gargravarr, 'in relation to it all?'

'Oh, yeah yeah.'

'But . . . what did you experience?'

Zaphod shrugged smugly.

'It just told me what I knew all the time. I'm a really terrific and great guy. Didn't I tell you, baby, I'm Zaphod Beeblebrox!'

His gaze passed over the machinery which powered the vortex and suddenly stopped, startled.

He breathed heavily.

'Hey,' he said, 'is that really a piece of fairy cake?'

He ripped the small piece of confectionery from the sensors with which it was surrounded.

'If I told you how much I needed this,' he said ravenously, 'I wouldn't have time to eat it.'

He ate it.

12

A short while later he was running across the plain in the direction of the ruined city.

The dank air wheezed heavily in his lungs and he frequently stumbled with the exhaustion he was still feeling. Night was beginning to fall too, and the rough ground was treacherous.

The elation of his recent experience was still with him though. The whole Universe. He had seen the whole Universe stretching to infinity around him – everything. And with it had come the clear and extraordinary knowledge that he was the most important thing in it. Having a conceited ego is one thing. Actually being told by a machine is another.

He didn't have time to reflect on this matter.

Gargravarr had told him that he would have to alert his masters as to what had happened, but that he was prepared to leave a decent interval before doing so. Enough time for Zaphod to make a break and find somewhere to hide.

What he was going to do he didn't know, but feeling that he was the most important person in the Universe gave him the confidence to believe that something would turn up.

Nothing else on this blighted planet could give him much grounds for optimism.

He ran on, and soon reached the outskirts of the abandoned city.

He walked along cracked and gaping roads riddled with scrawny weeds, the holes filled with rotting shoes. The buildings he passed were so crumbled and decrepit he thought it unsafe to enter any of them. Where could he hide? He hurried on.

After a while the remains of a wide sweeping road led off from the one down which he was walking, and at its end lay a vast low building, surrounded with sundry smaller ones, the whole surrounded by the remains of a perimeter barrier. The large main building still seemed reasonably solid, and Zaphod turned off to see if it might provide him with . . . well, with anything.

He approached the building. Along one side of it – the front it would seem since it faced a wide concreted apron area – were three gigantic doors, maybe sixty feet high. The far one of these was open, and towards this Zaphod ran.

Inside, all was gloom, dust and confusion. Giant cobwebs lay over everything. Part of the infrastructure of the building had collapsed, part of the rear wall had caved in, and a thick choking dust lay inches deep over the floor.

Through the heavy gloom huge shapes loomed, covered with debris.

The shapes were sometimes cylindrical, sometimes bulbous, sometimes like eggs, or rather cracked eggs. Most of them were split open or falling apart, some were mere skeletons.

They were all spacecraft, all derelict.

Zaphod wandered in frustration amongst the hulks. There was nothing here that remotely approached the serviceable. Even the mere vibration of his footsteps caused one precarious wreck to collapse further into itself.

Towards the rear of the building lay one old ship, slightly larger than the others, and buried beneath even deeper piles of dust and cobwebs. Its outline, however, seemed unbroken. Zaphod approached it with interest, and as he did so, he tripped over an old feedline.

He tried to toss the feedline aside, and to his surprise discovered that it was still connected to the ship.

To his utter astonishment he realized that the feedline was also humming slightly.

He stared at the ship in disbelief, and then back down at the feedline in his hands.

He tore off his jacket and threw it aside. Crawling along on his hands and knees he followed the feedline to the point where it connected with the ship. The connection was sound, and the slight humming vibration was more distinct.

His heart was beating fast. He wiped away some grime and laid an ear against the ship's side. He could hear only a faint, indeterminate noise.

He rummaged feverishly amongst the debris lying on the floor all about him and found a short length of tubing, and a non-biodegradable plastic cup. Out of this he fashioned a crude stethoscope and placed it against the side of the ship.

What he heard made his brains turn somersaults.

The voice said:

'Transtellar Cruise Lines would like to apologize to passengers for the continuing delay to this flight. We are currently awaiting the loading of our complement of small lemon-soaked paper napkins for your comfort, refreshment and hygiene during the journey. Meanwhile we thank you for your patience. The cabin crew will shortly be serving coffee and biscuits again.'

Zaphod staggered backwards, staring wildly at the ship.

He walked around for a few moments in a daze. In so doing he suddenly caught sight of a giant departure board still hanging, but by only one support, from the ceiling above him. It was covered with grime, but some of the figures were still discernible.

Zaphod's eyes searched amongst the figures, then made some brief calculations. His eyes widened.

'Nine hundred years . . .' he breathed to himself. That was how late the ship was.

Two minutes later he was on board.

As he stepped out of the airlock, the air that greeted him was cool and fresh – the air conditioning was still working.

The lights were still on.

He moved out of the small entrance chamber into a short narrow corridor and stepped nervously down it.

Suddenly a door opened and a figure stepped out in front of him.

'Please return to your seat, sir,' said the android stewardess and, turning her back on him, she walked on down the corridor in front of him.

When his heart had started beating again he followed her. She opened the door at the end of the corridor and walked through.

He followed her through the door.

They were now in the passenger compartment and Zaphod's heart stopped still again for a moment.

In every seat sat a passenger, strapped into his or her seat.

The passengers' hair was long and unkempt, their fingernails were long, the men wore beards.

All of them were quite clearly alive – but sleeping.

Zaphod had the creeping horrors.

He walked slowly down the aisle as in a dream. By the time he was halfway down the aisle, the stewardess had reached the other end. She turned and spoke.

'Good afternoon, ladies and gentlemen,' she said sweetly, 'thank you for bearing with us during this slight delay. We will be taking off as soon as we possibly can. If you would like to wake up now I will serve you coffee and biscuits.'

There was a slight hum.

At that moment, all the passengers awoke.

They awoke screaming and clawing at the straps and life-support systems that held them tightly in their seats. They screamed and bawled and hollered till Zaphod thought his ears would shatter.

They struggled and writhed as the stewardess patiently moved up the aisle placing a small cup of coffee and a packet of biscuits in front of each one of them.

Then one of them rose from his seat.

He turned and looked at Zaphod.

Zaphod's skin was crawling all over his body as if it was trying to get off. He turned and ran from the bedlam.

He plunged through the door and back into the corridor.

The man pursued him.

He raced in a frenzy to the end of the corridor, through the entrance chamber and beyond. He arrived on the flight deck, slammed and bolted the door behind him. He leant back against the door breathing hard.

Within seconds, a hand started beating on the door.

From somewhere on the flight deck a metallic voice addressed him.

'Passengers are not allowed on the flight deck. Please return to your seat, and wait for the ship to take off. Coffee and biscuits are being served. This is your autopilot speaking. Please return to your seat.'

Zaphod said nothing. He breathed hard, behind him, the hand continued to knock on the door.

'Please return to your seat,' repeated the autopilot. 'Passengers are not allowed on the flight deck.'

'I'm not a passenger,' panted Zaphod.

'Please return to your seat.'

'I am not a passenger!' shouted Zaphod again.

'Please return to your seat.'

'I am not a . . . hello, can you hear me?'

'Please return to your seat.'

'You're the autopilot?' said Zaphod.

'Yes,' said the voice from the flight console.

'You're in charge of this ship?'

'Yes,' said the voice again, 'there has been a delay. Passengers are to be kept temporarily in suspended animation, for their comfort and convenience. Coffee and biscuits are served every year, after which passengers are returned to suspended animation for their continued comfort and convenience. Departure will take place when the flight stores are complete. We apologize for the delay.'

Zaphod moved away from the door, on which the pounding had now ceased. He approached the flight console.

'Delay?' he cried. 'Have you seen the world outside this ship? It's a wasteland, a desert. Civilization's been and gone, man. There are no lemon-soaked paper napkins on the way from anywhere!'

'The statistical likelihood,' continued the autopilot primly, 'is that other civilizations will arise. There will one day be lemon-soaked paper napkins. Till then there will be a short delay. Please return to your seat.'

'But . . .'

But at that moment the door opened. Zaphod span round to see the man who had pursued him standing there. He carried a large briefcase. He was smartly dressed, and his hair was short. He had no beard and no long fingernails.

'Zaphod Beeblebrox,' he said, 'my name is Zarniwoop. I believe you wanted to see me.'

Zaphod Beeblebrox wittered. His mouths said foolish things. He dropped into a chair.

'Oh man, oh man, where did you spring from?' he said.

'I have been waiting here for you,' he said in a businesslike tone.

He put the briefcase down and sat in another chair.

'I am glad you followed instructions,' he said, 'I was a bit nervous that you might have left my office by the door rather than the window. Then you would have been in trouble.'

Zaphod shook his heads at him and burbled.

'When you entered the door of my office, you entered my electronically synthesized Universe,' he explained, 'if you had left by the door you would have been back in the real one. The artificial one works from here.'

He patted the briefcase smugly.

Zaphod glared at him with resentment and loathing.

'What's the difference?' he muttered.

'Nothing,' said Zarniwoop, 'they are identical. Oh – except that I think the Frogstar Fighters are grey in the real Universe.'

'What's going on?' spat Zaphod.

'Simple,' said Zarniwoop. His self-assurance and smugness made Zaphod seethe.

'Very simple,' repeated Zarniwoop, 'I discovered the co-ordinates at which this man could be found – the man who rules the Universe and discovered that his world was protected by an Unprobability Field. To protect my secret – and myself – I retreated to the safety of this totally artificial Universe and hid myself away in a forgotten cruise liner. I was secure. Meanwhile, you and I . . .'

'You and *I*?' said Zaphod angrily. 'You mean I knew you?'

'Yes,' said Zarniwoop, 'we knew each other well.'

'I had no taste,' said Zaphod and resumed a sullen silence.

'Meanwhile, you and I arranged that you would steal the Improbability Drive ship – the only one which could reach the ruler's world – and bring it to me here. This you have now done I trust, and I congratulate you.' He smiled a tight little smile which Zaphod wanted to hit with a brick.

'Oh, and in case you were wondering,' added Zarniwoop, 'this Universe was created specifically for you to come to. You are therefore the most important person in this Universe. You would never,' he said with an even more brickable smile, 'have survived the Total Perspective Vortex in the real one. Shall we go?'

'Where?' said Zaphod sullenly. He felt collapsed.

'To your ship. The *Heart of Gold*. You did bring it, I trust?'

'No.'

'Where is your jacket?'

Zaphod looked at him in mystification.

'My jacket? I took it off. It's outside.'

'Good, we will go and find it.'

Zarniwoop stood up and gestured to Zaphod to follow him.

Out in the entrance chamber again, they could hear the screams of the passengers being fed coffee and biscuits.

'It has not been a pleasant experience waiting for you,' said Zarniwoop.

'Not pleasant for *you*!' bawled Zaphod. 'How do you think . . .'

Zarniwoop held up a silencing finger as the hatchway swung open. A few feet away from them they could see Zaphod's jacket lying in the debris.

'A very remarkable and very powerful ship,' said Zarniwoop, 'watch.'

As they watched, the pocket on the jacket suddenly bulged. It split, it ripped. The small metal model of the

Heart of Gold that Zaphod had been bewildered to discover in his pocket was growing.

It grew, it continued to grow. It reached, after two minutes, its full size.

'At an Improbability Level,' said Zarniwoop, 'of . . . oh I don't know, but something very large.'

Zaphod swayed.

'You mean I had it with me all the time?'

Zarniwoop smiled. He lifted up his briefcase and opened it.

He twisted a single switch inside it.

'Goodbye artificial Universe,' he said, 'hello real one!'

The scene before them shimmered briefly – and reappeared exactly as before.

'You see?' said Zarniwoop. 'Exactly the same.'

'You mean,' repeated Zaphod tautly, 'that I had it with me all the time?'

'Oh yes,' said Zarniwoop, 'of course. That was the whole point.'

'That's it,' said Zaphod, 'you can count me out, from here-on in you can count me out. I've had all I want of this. You play your own games.'

'I'm afraid you cannot leave,' said Zarniwoop, 'you are entwined in the Improbability Field. You cannot escape.'

He smiled the smile that Zaphod had wanted to hit and this time Zaphod hit it.

13

Ford Prefect bounded up to the bridge of the *Heart of Gold*.

'Trillian! Arthur!' he shouted. 'It's working! The ship's reactivated!'

Trillian and Arthur were asleep on the floor.

'Come on you guys, we're going, we're off,' he said kicking them awake.

'Hi there, guys!' twittered the computer. 'It's really great to be back with you again, I can tell you, and I just want to say that—'

'Shut up,' said Ford, 'and tell us where the hell we are.'

'Frogstar World B, and man it's a dump,' said Zaphod running on to the bridge. 'Hi, guys, you must be so amazingly glad to see me you can't even find words to tell me what a cool frood I am.'

'What a what?' said Arthur blearily, picking himself up from the floor and not taking any of this in.

'I know how you feel,' said Zaphod. 'I'm so great even I get tongue-tied talking to myself. Hey, it's good to see you, Trillian, Ford, Monkeyman. Hey, er, computer . . .?'

'Hi there, Mr Beeblebrox, sir, sure is a great honour to—'

'Shut up and get us out of here, fast fast fast.'

'Sure thing, fella, where do you want to go?'

'Anywhere, doesn't matter,' shouted Zaphod. 'Yes it does!' he said again. 'We want to go to the nearest place to eat!'

'Sure thing,' said the computer happily and a massive explosion rocked the bridge.

When Zarniwoop entered a minute or so later with a black eye, he regarded the four wisps of smoke with interest.

14

Four inert bodies sank through spinning blackness. Consciousness had died, cold oblivion pulled the bodies down and down into the pit of unbeing. The roar of silence echoed dismally around them and they sank at last into a dark and bitter sea of heaving red that slowly engulfed them, seemingly for ever.

After what seemed an eternity the seas receded and left them lying on a cold hard shore, the flotsam and jetsam of the stream of Life, the Universe and Everything.

Cold spasms shook them, lights danced sickeningly around them. The cold hard shore tipped and span and then stood still. It shone darkly – it was a very highly polished cold hard shore.

A green blur watched them disapprovingly.

It coughed.

'Good evening, madam, gentlemen,' it said, 'do you have a reservation?'

Ford Prefect's consciousness snapped back like elastic, making his brain smart. He looked up woozily at the green blur.

'Reservation?' he said weakly.

'Yes, sir,' said the green blur.

'Do you need a reservation for the afterlife?'

In so far as it is possible for a green blur to arch its eyebrows disdainfully, this is what the green blur now did.

'Afterlife, sir?' it said.

Arthur Dent was grappling with his consciousness the way one grapples with a lost bar of soap in the bath.

'Is this the afterlife?' he stammered.

'Well, I assume so,' said Ford Prefect trying to work

out which way was up. He tested the theory that it must lie in the opposite direction from the cold hard shore on which he was lying, and staggered to what he hoped were his feet.

'I mean,' he said, swaying gently, 'there's no way we could have survived that blast, is there?'

'No,' muttered Arthur. He had raised himself on to his elbows but it didn't seem to improve things. He slumped down again.

'No,' said Trillian, standing up, 'no way at all.'

A dull hoarse gurgling sound came from the floor. It was Zaphod Beeblebrox attempting to speak.

'I certainly didn't survive,' he gurgled, 'I was a total goner. Wham bang and that was it.'

'Yeah, thanks to you,' said Ford, 'we didn't stand a chance. We must have been blown to bits. Arms, legs everywhere.'

'Yeah,' said Zaphod struggling noisily to his feet.

'If the lady and gentlemen would care to order drinks . . .' said the green blur, hovering impatiently beside them.

'Kerpow, splat,' continued Zaphod, 'instantaneously zonked into our component molecules. Hey, Ford,' he said, identifying one of the slowly solidifying blurs around him, 'did you get that thing of your whole life flashing before you?'

'You got that too?' said Ford. 'Your whole life?'

'Yeah,' said Zaphod, 'at least I assume it was mine. I spend a lot of time out of my skulls, you know.'

He looked around him at the various shapes that were at last becoming proper shapes instead of vague and wobbling shapeless shapes.

'So . . .' he said.

'So what?' said Ford.

'So here we are,' said Zaphod hesitantly, 'lying dead . . .'

'Standing,' Trillian corrected him.

'Er, standing dead,' continued Zaphod, 'in this desolate . . .'

'Restaurant,' said Arthur Dent who had got to his feet and could now, much to his surprise, see clearly. That is to say, the thing that surprised him was not that he could see, but what he could see.

'Here we are,' continued Zaphod doggedly, 'standing dead in this desolate . . .'

'Five star,' said Trillian.

'Restaurant,' concluded Zaphod.

'Odd, isn't it?' said Ford.

'Er, yeah.'

'Nice chandeliers though,' said Trillian.

They looked about themselves in bemusement.

'It's not so much an afterlife,' said Arthur, 'more a sort of après vie.'

The chandeliers were in fact a little on the flashy side and the low vaulted ceiling from which they hung would not, in an ideal Universe, have been painted in that particular shade of deep turquoise, and even if it had been it wouldn't have been highlighted by concealed moodlighting. This is not, however, an ideal Universe, as was further evidenced by the eye-crossing patterns of the inlaid marble floor, and the way in which the fronting for the eighty-yard long marble-topped bar had been made. The fronting for the eighty-yard long marble-topped bar had been made by stitching together nearly twenty thousand Antarean Mosaic Lizard skins, despite the fact that the twenty thousand lizards concerned had needed them to keep their insides in.

A few smartly dressed creatures were lounging casually at the bar or relaxing in the richly coloured body-hugging seats that were deployed here and there about the bar area. A young Vl'Hurg officer and his green ssteaming young lady passed through the large smoked glass doors at the far end of the bar into the dazzling light of the main body of the restaurant beyond.

Behind Arthur was a large curtained bay window. He pulled aside the corner of the curtain and looked out at a bleak and drear landscape, grey, pockmarked and dismal, a landscape which under normal circumstances would have given Arthur the creeping horrors. These were not, however, normal circumstances, for the thing that froze his blood and made his skin try to crawl up his back and off the top off his head was the sky. The sky was . . .

An attendant flunkey politely drew the curtain back into place.

'All in good time, sir,' he said.

Zaphod's eyes flashed.

'Hey, hang about, you dead guys,' he said, 'I think we're missing some ultra-important thing here you know. Something somebody said and we missed it.'

Arthur was profoundly relieved to turn his attention from what he had just seen.

He said, 'I said it was a sort of après . . .'

'Yeah, and don't you wish you hadn't?' said Zaphod, 'Ford?'

'I said it was odd.'

'Yeah, shrewd but dull, perhaps it was—'

'Perhaps,' interrupted the green blur who had by this time resolved into the shape of a small wizened dark-suited green waiter, 'perhaps you would care to discuss the matter over drinks . . .'

'Drinks!' cried Zaphod. 'That was it! See what you miss if you don't stay alert.'

'Indeed, sir,' said the waiter patiently. 'If the lady and gentlemen would care to take drinks before dinner . . .'

'Dinner!' Zaphod exclaimed with passion. 'Listen,

little green person, my stomach could take you home and cuddle you all night for the mere idea.'

'. . . and the Universe,' continued the waiter, determined not to be deflected on his home stretch, 'will explode later for your pleasure.'

Ford's head swivelled slowly towards him. He spoke with feeling.

'Wow,' he said. 'What sort of drinks do you serve in this place?'

The waiter laughed a polite little waiter's laugh.

'Ah,' he said. 'I think sir has perhaps misunderstood me.'

'Oh, I hope not,' breathed Ford.

The waiter coughed a polite little waiter's cough.

'It is not unusual for our customers to be a little disorientated by the time journey,' he said, 'so if I might suggest . . .'

'Time journey?' said Zaphod.

'Time journey?' said Ford.

'Time journey?' said Trillian.

'You mean this isn't the afterlife?' said Arthur.

The waiter smiled a polite little waiter's smile. He had almost exhausted his polite little waiter repertoire and would soon be slipping into his role of a rather tight-lipped and sarcastic little waiter.

'Afterlife, sir?' he said. 'No, sir.'

'And we're not dead?' said Arthur.

The waiter tightened his lips.

'Aha, ha,' he said. 'Sir is most evidently alive, otherwise I would not attempt to serve sir.'

In an extraordinary gesture which it is pointless attempting to describe, Zaphod Beeblebrox slapped both his foreheads with two of his arms and one of his thighs with the other.

'Hey, guys,' he said, 'this is crazy. We did it. We finally got to where we were going. This is Milliways!'

'Milliways!' said Ford.

'Yes, sir,' said the waiter, laying on the patience with a trowel, 'this is Milliways – the Restaurant at the End of the Universe.'

'End of what?' said Arthur.

'In just a few minutes, sir,' said the waiter. He took a deep breath. He didn't need to do this since his body was supplied with the peculiar assortment of gases it required for survival from a small intravenous device strapped to his leg. There are times, however, when whatever your metabolism you have to take a deep breath.

'Now, if you would care to order your drinks at last,' he said, 'I will then show you to your table.'

Zaphod grinned two manic grins, sauntered over to the bar and bought most of it.

15

The Restaurant at the End of the Universe is one of the most extraordinary ventures in the entire history of catering. It has been built on the fragmented remains of . . . it *will* be built on the fragmented . . . that is to say it will have been built by this time, and indeed has been—

One of the major problems encountered in time travel is not that of accidentally becoming your own father or mother. There is no problem involved in becoming your own father or mother that a broadminded and well-adjusted family can't cope with. There is also no problem about changing the course of history – the course of history does not change because it all fits together like a jigsaw. All the important changes have happened before the things they were supposed to change and it all sorts itself out in the end.

The major problem is quite simply one of grammar, and the main work to consult in this matter is Dr Dan Streetmentioner's *Time Traveller's Handbook of 1001 Tense Formations*. It will tell you for instance how to describe something that was about to happen to you in the past before you avoided it by time-jumping forward two days in order to avoid it. The event will be described differently according to whether you are talking about it from the standpoint of your own natural time, from a time in the further future, or a time in the further past and is further complicated by the possibility of conducting conversations whilst you are actually travelling from one time to another with the intention of becoming your own mother or father.

Most readers get as far as the Future Semi-Conditionally Modified Subinverted Plagal Past Subjunctive Intentional before giving up: and in fact in later editions of the book all the pages beyond this point have been left blank to save on printing costs.

The Hitchhiker's Guide to the Galaxy skips lightly over this tangle of academic abstraction, pausing only to note that the term 'Future Perfect' has been abandoned since it was discovered not to be.

To resume:

The Restaurant at the End of the Universe is one of the most extraordinary ventures in the entire history of catering.

It is built on the fragmented remains of an eventually ruined planet which is (wioll haven be) enclosed in a vast time bubble and projected forward in time to the precise moment of the End of the Universe.

This is, many would say, impossible.

In it, guests take (willan on-take) their places at table and eat (willan on-eat) sumptuous meals whilst watching (willing watchen) the whole of creation explode around them.

This, many would say, is equally impossible.

You can arrive (mayan arrivan on-when) for any sitting you like without prior (late fore-when) reservation because you can book retrospectively, as it were, when you return to your own time. (You can have on-book haventa forewhen presooning returningwenta retrohome.)

This is, many would not insist, absolutely impossible.

At the Restaurant you can meet and dine with (mayan meetan con with dinan on-when) a fascinating cross-section of the entire population of space and time.

This, it can be explained patiently, is also impossible.

You can visit it as many times as you like (mayan on-visit re-onvisiting ... and so on – for further tense correction consult Dr Streetmentioner's book) and be sure of never meeting yourself, because of the embarrassment this usually causes.

This, even if the rest were true, which it isn't, is patently impossible, say the doubters.

All you have to do is deposit one penny in a savings account in your own era, and when you arrive at the End of Time the operation of compound interest means that the fabulous cost of your meal has been paid for.

This, many claim, is not merely impossible but clearly insane, which is why the advertising executives of the star system of Bastablon came up with this slogan: 'If you've done six impossible things this morning, why not round it off with breakfast at Milliways, the Restaurant at the End of the Universe?'

16

At the bar, Zaphod was rapidly becoming as tired as a newt. His heads knocked together and his smiles were coming out of synch. He was miserably happy.

'Zaphod,' said Ford, 'whilst you're still capable of speech, would you care to tell me what the photon happened? Where have you been? Where have we been? Small matter, but I'd like it cleared up.'

Zaphod's left head sobered up, leaving his right to sink further into the obscurity of drink.

'Yeah,' he said, 'I've been around. They want me to find the man who rules the Universe, but I don't care to meet him. I believe the man can't cook.'

His left head watched his right head saying this and then nodded.

'True,' it said, 'have another drink.'

Ford had another Pan Galactic Gargle Blaster, the drink which has been described as the alcoholic equivalent of a mugging – expensive and bad for the head. Whatever had happened, Ford decided, he didn't really care too much.

'Listen, Ford,' said Zaphod, 'everything's cool and froody.'

'You mean everything's under control.'

'No,' said Zaphod, 'I do not mean everything's under control. That would not be cool and froody. If you want to know what happened let's just say I had the whole situation in my pocket. OK?'

Ford shrugged.

Zaphod giggled into his drink. It frothed up over the side of the glass and started to eat its way into the marble bar top.

A wild-skinned sky-gypsy approached them and played electric violin at them until Zaphod gave him a lot of money and he agreed to go away again.

The gypsy approached Arthur and Trillian sitting in another part of the bar.

'I don't know what this place is,' said Arthur, 'but I think it gives me the creeps.'

'Have another drink,' said Trillian. 'Enjoy yourself.'

'Which?' said Arthur. 'The two are mutually exclusive.'

'Poor Arthur, you're not really cut out for this life, are you?'

'You call this life?'

'You're beginning to sound like Marvin.'

'Marvin's the clearest thinker I know. How do you think we make this violinist go away?'

The waiter approached.

'Your table is ready,' he said.

Seen from the outside, which it never is, the Restaurant resembles a giant glittering starfish beached on a forgotten rock. Each of its arms house the bars, the kitchens, the force-field generators which protect the entire structure and the decayed hunk of planet on which it sits, and the Time Turbines which slowly rock the whole affair backwards and forwards across the crucial moment.

In the centre sits the gigantic golden dome, almost a complete globe, and it was into this area that Zaphod, Ford, Arthur and Trillian now passed.

At least five tons of glitter alone had gone into it before them, and covered every available surface. The other surfaces were not available because they were already encrusted with jewels, precious sea shells from Santraginus, gold leaf, mosaic tiles, lizard skins and a million unidentifiable embellishments and decorations. Glass glittered, silver shone, gold gleamed, Arthur Dent goggled.

'Wowee,' said Zaphod. 'Zappo.'

'Incredible!' breathed Arthur. 'The people . . . ! The things . . . !'

'The things,' said Ford Prefect quietly, 'are also people.'

'The people . . .' resumed Arthur, 'the . . . other people . . .'

'The lights . . . !' said Trillian.

'The tables . . . !' said Arthur.

'The clothes . . . !' said Trillian.

The waiter thought they sounded like a couple of bailiffs.

'The End of the Universe is very popular,' said Zaphod threading his way unsteadily through the throng of tables, some made of marble, some of rich ultra-mahogany, some even of platinum, and at each a party of exotic creatures chatting amongst themselves and studying menus.

'People like to dress up for it,' continued Zaphod. 'Gives it a sense of occasion.'

The tables were fanned out in a large circle around a central stage area where a small band were playing light music, at least a thousand tables was Arthur's guess, and interspersed amongst them were swaying palms, hissing fountains, grotesque statuary, in short all the paraphernalia common to the restaurants where little expense had been spared to give the impression that no expense has been spared. Arthur glanced round, half expecting to see someone making an American Express commercial.

Zaphod lurched into Ford, who lurched back into Zaphod.

'Wowee,' said Zaphod.

'Zappo,' said Ford.

'My great-granddaddy must have really screwed up the computer's works, you know,' said Zaphod. 'I told it to take us to the nearest place to eat and it sends us to the End of the Universe. Remind me to be nice to it one day.'

He paused.

'Hey, everybody's here you know. Everybody who was anybody.'

'Was?' said Arthur.

'At the End of the Universe you have to use the past tense a lot,' said Zaphod, ''cos everything's been done, you know. Hi, guys,' he called out to a nearby party of giant iguana life-forms, 'how did you do?'

'Is that Zaphod Beeblebrox?' asked one iguana of another iguana.

'I think so,' replied the second iguana.

'Well, doesn't that just take the biscuit,' said the first iguana.

'Funny old thing, life,' said the second iguana.

'It's what you make it,' said the first and they lapsed back into silence. They were waiting for the greatest show in the Universe.

'Hey, Zaphod,' said Ford, grabbing for his arm and, on account of the third Pan Galactic Gargle Blaster, missing. He pointed a swaying finger.

'There's an old mate of mine,' he said. 'Hotblack Desiato! See the man at the platinum table with the platinum suit on?'

Zaphod tried to follow Ford's finger with his eyes but it made him feel dizzy. Finally he saw.

'Oh yeah,' he said, then recognition came a moment later. 'Hey,' he said, 'did that guy ever make it megabig! Wow, bigger than the biggest thing ever. Other than me.'

'Who's he supposed to be?' asked Trillian.

'Hotblack Desiato?' said Zaphod in astonishment. 'You don't know? You never heard of Disaster Area?'

'No,' said Trillian, who hadn't.

'The biggest,' said Ford, 'loudest . . .'

'Richest . . .' suggested Zaphod.

'. . . rock band in the history of . . .' He searched for the word.

'. . . history itself,' said Zaphod.

'No,' said Trillian.

'Zowee,' said Zaphod, 'here we are at the End of the Universe and you haven't even lived yet. Did you miss out.'

He led her off to where the waiter had been waiting all this time at the table. Arthur followed them feeling very lost and alone.

Ford waded off through the throng to renew an old acquaintance.

'Hey, er, Hotblack,' he called out, 'how you doing? Great to see you, big boy, how's the noise? You're looking great, really very, very fat and unwell. Amazing.' He slapped the man on the back and was mildly surprised that it seemed to elicit no response. The Pan Galactic Gargle Blasters swilling round inside him told him to plunge on regardless.

'Remember the old days?' he said. 'We used to hang out, right? The Bistro Illegal, remember? Slim's Throat Emporium? The Evildrome Boozarama, great days, eh?'

Hotblack Desiato offered no opinion as to whether they were great days or not. Ford was not perturbed.

'And when we were hungry we'd pose as public health inspectors, you remember that? And go around confiscating meals and drinks, right? Till we got food poisoning. Oh, and then there were the long nights of talking and drinking in those smelly rooms above the Café Lou in Gretchen Town, New Betel, and you were always in the next room trying to write songs on your ajuitar and we all hated them. And you said you didn't care, and we said we did because we hated them so much.' Ford's eyes were beginning to mist over.

'And you said you didn't want to be a star,' he continued, wallowing in nostalgia, 'because you despised the star system. And we said, Hadra and Sulijoo and me, that we didn't think you had the option. And what do you do now? You *buy* star systems!'

He turned and solicited the attention of those at nearby tables.

'Here,' he said 'is a man who *buys* star systems!'

Hotblack Desiato made no attempt either to confirm or deny this fact, and the attention of the temporary audience waned rapidly.

'I think someone's drunk,' muttered a purple bush-like being into his wine glass.

Ford staggered slightly, and sat down heavily on the chair facing Hotblack Desiato.

'What's that number you do?' he said, unwisely grabbing at a bottle for support and tipping it over – into a nearby glass as it happened. Not to waste a happy accident, he drained the glass.

'That really huge number,' he continued, 'how does it go? "Bwarm! Bwarm! Baderr!!" something, and in the stage act you do it ends up with this ship crashing right into the sun, and you actually *do* it!'

Ford crashed his fist into his other hand to illustrate this feat graphically. He knocked the bottle over again.

'Ship! Sun! Wham bang!' he cried. 'I mean forget lasers and stuff, you guys are into solar flares and *real* sunburn! Oh, and terrible songs.'

His eyes followed the stream of liquid glugging out

of the bottle on to the table. Something ought to be done about it, he thought.

'Hey, you want a drink?' he said. It began to sink into his squelching mind that something was missing from this reunion, and that the missing something was in some way connected with the fact that the fat man sitting opposite him in the platinum suit and the silvery trilby had not yet said 'Hi, Ford,' or 'Great to see you after all this time,' or in fact anything at all. More to the point he had not yet even moved.

'Hotblack?' said Ford.

A large meaty hand landed on his shoulder from behind and pushed him aside. He slid gracelessly off his seat and peered upwards to see if he could spot the owner of this discourteous hand. The owner was not hard to spot, on account of his being something of the order of seven feet tall and not slightly built with it. In fact he was built the way one builds leather sofas, shiny, lumpy and with lots of solid stuffing. The suit into which the man's body had been stuffed looked as if its only purpose in life was to demonstrate how difficult it was to get this sort of body into a suit. The face had the texture of an orange and the colour of an apple, but there the resemblance to anything sweet ended.

'Kid . . .' said a voice which emerged from the man's mouth as if it had been having a really rough time down in his chest.

'Er, yeah?' said Ford conversationally. He staggered back to his feet again and was disappointed that the top of his head didn't come further up the man's body.

'Beat it,' said the man.

'Oh yeah,' said Ford, wondering how wise he was being, 'and who are you?'

The man considered this for a moment. He wasn't used to being asked this sort of question. Nevertheless, after a while he came up with an answer.

'I'm the guy who's telling you to beat it,' he said, 'before you get it beaten for you.'

'Now listen,' said Ford nervously – he wished his head would stop spinning, settle down and get to grips with the situation. 'Now listen,' he continued, 'I am one of Hotblack's oldest friends and . . .'

He glanced at Hotblack Desiato, who still hadn't moved so much as an eyelash.

'. . . and . . .' said Ford again, wondering what would be a good word to say after 'and'.

The large man came up with a whole sentence to go after 'and'. He said it.

'And I am Mr Desiato's bodyguard,' it went, 'and I am responsible for his body, and I am not responsible for yours, so take it away before it gets damaged.'

'Now wait a minute,' said Ford.

'No minutes!' boomed the bodyguard. 'No waiting! Mr Desiato speaks to no one!'

'Well perhaps you'd let him say what he thinks about the matter himself,' said Ford.

'He speaks to no one!' bellowed the bodyguard.

Ford glanced anxiously at Hotblack again and was forced to admit to himself that the bodyguard seemed to have the facts on his side. There was still not the slightest sign of movement, let alone keen interest in Ford's welfare.

'Why?' said Ford. 'What's the matter with him?'

The bodyguard told him.

17

The Hitchhiker's Guide to the Galaxy notes that Disaster Area, a plutonium rock band from the Gagrakacka Mind

Zones, are generally held to be not only the loudest rock band in the Galaxy, but in fact the loudest noise of any kind at all. Regular concert-goers judge that the best sound is usually to be heard from within large concrete bunkers some thirty-seven miles from the stage, whilst the musicians themselves play their instruments by remote control from within a heavily insulated spaceship which stays in orbit around the planet – or more frequently around a completely different planet.

Their songs are on the whole very simple and mostly follow the familiar theme of boy-being meets girl-being beneath a silvery moon, which then explodes for no adequately explored reason.

Many worlds have now banned their act altogether, sometimes for artistic reasons, but most commonly because the band's public address system contravenes local strategic arms limitations treaties.

This has not, however, stopped their earnings from pushing back the boundaries of pure hypermathematics, and their chief research accountant has recently been appointed Professor of Neomathematics at the University of Maximegalon, in recognition of both his General and his Special Theories of Disaster Area Tax Returns, in which he proves that the whole fabric of the space – time continuum is not merely curved, it is in fact totally bent.

Ford staggered back to the table where Zaphod, Arthur and Trillian were sitting waiting for the fun to begin.

'Gotta have some food,' said Ford.

'Hi, Ford,' said Zaphod, 'you speak to the big noise boy?'

Ford waggled his head noncommitally.

'Hotblack? I sort of spoke to him, yeah.'

'What'd he say?'

'Well, not a lot really. He's . . . er . . .'

'Yeah?'

'He's spending a year dead for tax reasons. I've got to sit down.'

He sat down.

The waiter approached.

'Would you like to see the menu,' he said, 'or would you like to meet the Dish of the Day?'

'Huh?' said Ford.

'Huh?' said Arthur.

'Huh?' said Trillian.

'That's cool,' said Zaphod, 'we'll meet the meat.'

In a small room in one of the arms of the restaurant complex a tall, thin, gangling figure pulled aside a curtain and oblivion looked him in the face.

It was not a pretty face, perhaps because oblivion had looked him in it so many times. It was too long, for a start, the eyes too sunken and hooded, the cheeks too hollow, his lips were too thin and too long, and when they parted his teeth looked too much like a recently polished bay window. The hands that held the curtain were long and thin too: they were also cold. They lay lightly along the folds of the curtain and gave the impression that if he didn't watch them like a hawk they would crawl away of their own accord and do something unspeakable in a corner.

He let the curtain drop and the terrible light that had played on his features went off to play somewhere more healthy. He prowled around his small chamber like a mantis contemplating an evening's preying, finally settling on a rickety chair by a trestle table, where he leafed through a few sheets of jokes.

A bell rang.

He pushed the thin sheaf of papers aside and stood

up. His hands brushed limply over some of the one million rainbow-coloured sequins with which his jacket was festooned, and he was gone through the door.

In the restaurant the lights dimmed, the band quickened its pace, a single spotlight stabbed down into the darkness of the stairway that led up to the centre of the stage.

Up the stairs bounded a tall brilliantly coloured figure. He burst on to the stage, tripped lightly up to the microphone, removed it from its stand with one swoop of his long thin hand and stood for a moment bowing left and right to the audience acknowledging their applause and displaying to them his bay window. He waved to his particular friends in the audience even though there weren't any there, and waited for the applause to die down.

He held up his hand and smiled a smile that stretched not merely from ear to ear, but seemed to extend some way beyond the mere confines of his face.

'Thank you, ladies and gentlemen!' he cried. 'Thank you very much. Thank you so much.'

He eyed them with a twinkling eye.

'Ladies and gentlemen,' he said, 'the Universe as we know it has now been in existence for over one hundred and seventy thousand million billion years and will be ending in a little over half an hour. So, welcome one and all to Milliways, the Restaurant at the End of the Universe!'

With a gesture he deftly conjured another round of spontaneous applause. With another gesture he cut it.

'I am your host for tonight,' he said, 'my name is Max Quordlepleen . . .' (Everybody knew this, his act was famous throughout the known Galaxy, but he said it for the fresh applause it generated, which he acknowledged with a disclaiming smile and wave.)' . . . and I've just come straight from the very very other end of time, where I've been hosting a show at the Big Bank Burger Bar – where I can tell you we had a very exciting evening, ladies and gentlemen – and I will be with you right through this historic occasion, the End of History itself!'

Another burst of applause died away quickly as the lights dimmed down further. On every table candles ignited themselves spontaneously, eliciting a slight gasp from all the diners and wreathing them in a thousand tiny flickering lights and a million intimate shadows. A tremor of excitement thrilled through the darkened restaurant as the vast golden dome above them began very very slowly to dim, to darken, to fade.

Max's voice was hushed as he continued.

'So, ladies and gentlemen,' he breathed, 'the candles are lit, the band plays softly, and as the force-shielded dome above us fades into transparency, revealing a dark and sullen sky hung heavy with the ancient light of livid swollen stars, I can see we're all in for a fabulous evening's apocalypse!'

Even the soft tootling of the band faded away as stunned shock descended on all those who had not seen this sight before.

A monstrous, grisly light poured in on them,

– a hideous light,

– a boiling, pestilential light,

– a light that would have disfigured hell.

The Universe was coming to an end.

For a few interminable seconds the restaurant span silently through the raging void. Then Max spoke again.

'For those of you who ever hoped to see the light at the end of the tunnel,' he said, 'this is it.'

The band struck up again.

'Thank you, ladies and gentlemen,' cried Max, 'I'll be back with you again in just a moment, and meanwhile I leave you in the very capable hands of Mr Reg Nullify and his Cataclysmic Combo. Big hand please ladies and gentlemen for Reg and the boys!'

The baleful turmoil of the skies continued.

Hesitantly the audience began to clap and after a moment or so normal conversation resumed. Max began his round of the tables, swapping jokes, shouting with laughter, earning his living.

A large dairy animal approached Zaphod Beeblebrox's table, a large fat meaty quadruped of the bovine type with large watery eyes, small horns and what might almost have been an ingratiating smile on its lips.

'Good evening,' it lowed and sat back heavily on its haunches, 'I am the main Dish of the Day. May I interest you in parts of my body?' It harrumphed and gurgled a bit, wriggled its hind quarters into a more comfortable position and gazed peacefully at them.

Its gaze was met by looks of startled bewilderment from Arthur and Trillian, a resigned shrug from Ford Prefect and naked hunger from Zaphod Beeblebrox.

'Something off the shoulder, perhaps,' suggested the animal, 'braised in a white wine sauce?'

'Er, *your* shoulder?' said Arthur in a horrified whisper.

'But naturally my shoulder, sir,' mooed the animal contentedly, 'nobody else's is mine to offer.'

Zaphod leapt to his feet and started prodding and feeling the animal's shoulder appreciatively.

'Or the rump is very good,' murmured the animal. 'I've been exercising it and eating plenty of grain, so there's a lot of good meat there.' It gave a mellow grunt, gurgled again and started to chew the cud. It swallowed the cud again.

'Or a casserole of me, perhaps?' it added.

'You mean this animal actually wants us to eat it?' whispered Trillian to Ford.

'Me?' said Ford, with a glazed look in his eyes. 'I don't mean anything.'

'That's absolutely horrible,' exclaimed Arthur, 'the most revolting thing I've ever heard.'

'What's the problem, Earthman?' said Zaphod, now transfering his attention to the animal's enormous rump.

'I just don't want to eat an animal that's standing there inviting me to,' said Arthur, 'it's heartless.'

'Better than eating an animal that doesn't want to be eaten,' said Zaphod.

'That's not the point,' Arthur protested. Then he thought about it for a moment. 'All right,' he said, 'maybe it is the point. I don't care, I'm not going to think about it now. I'll just . . . er . . .'

The Universe raged about him in its death throes.

'I think I'll just have a green salad,' he muttered.

'May I urge you to consider my liver?' asked the animal. 'It must be very rich and tender by now, I've been force-feeding myself for months.'

'A green salad,' said Arthur emphatically.

'A green salad?' said the animal, rolling his eyes disapprovingly at Arthur.

'Are you going to tell me,' said Arthur, 'that I shouldn't have green salad?'

'Well,' said the animal, 'I know many vegetables that are very clear on that point. Which is why it was eventually decided to cut through the whole tangled problem and breed an animal that actually wanted to be eaten and was capable of saying so clearly and distinctly. And here I am.'

It managed a very slight bow.

'Glass of water, please,' said Arthur.

'Look,' said Zaphod, 'we want to eat, we don't want to make a meal of the issues. Four rare steaks please, and hurry. We haven't eaten in five hundred and seventy-six thousand million years.'

The animal staggered to its feet. It gave a mellow gurgle.

'A very wise choice, sir, if I may say so. Very good,' it said, 'I'll just nip off and shoot myself.'

He turned and gave a friendly wink to Arthur.

'Don't worry, sir,' he said, 'I'll be very humane.'

It waddled unhurriedly off to the kitchen.

A matter of minutes later the waiter arrived with four huge steaming steaks. Zaphod and Ford wolfed straight into them without a second's hesitation. Trillian paused, then shrugged and started into hers.

Arthur stared at his feeling slightly ill.

'Hey, Earthman,' said Zaphod with a malicious grin on the face that wasn't stuffing itself, 'what's eating you?'

And the band played on.

All around the restaurant people and things relaxed and chatted. The air was filled with talk of this and that, and with the mingled scents of exotic plants, extravagant foods and insidious wines. For an infinite number of miles in every direction the universal cataclysm was gathering to a stupefying climax. Glancing at his watch, Max returned to the stage with a flourish.

'And now, ladies and gentlemen,' he beamed, 'is everyone having one last wonderful time?'

'Yes,' called out the sort of people who call out 'yes' when comedians ask them if they're having a wonderful time.

'That's wonderful,' enthused Max, 'absolutely wonderful. And as the photon storms gather in swirling crowds around us, preparing to tear apart the last of the red hot suns, I know you're all going to settle back and enjoy with me what I know we will all find an immensely exciting and terminal experience.'

He paused. He caught the audience with a glittering eye.

'Believe me, ladies and gentlemen,' he said, 'there is nothing penultimate about this one.'

He paused again. Tonight his timing was immaculate. Time after time he had done this show, night after night. Not that the word night had any meaning here at the extremity of time. All there was was the endless repetition of the final moment, as the restaurant rocked slowly forward over the brink of time's furthest edge – and back again. This 'night' was good though, the audience was writhing in the palm of his sickly hand. His voice dropped. They had to strain to hear him.

'This,' he said, 'really is the absolute end, the final chilling desolation, in which the whole majestic sweep of creation becomes extinct. This, ladies and gentlemen, is the proverbial "it".'

He dropped his voice still lower. In the stillness, a fly would not have dared clear its throat.

'After this,' he said, 'there is nothing. Void. Emptiness. Oblivion. Absolute nothing . . .'

His eyes glittered again – or did they twinkle?

'Nothing . . . except of course for the sweet trolley, and a fine selection of Aldebaran liqueurs!'

The band gave him a music sting. He wished they wouldn't, he didn't need it, not an artist of his calibre. He could play the audience like his own musical instrument. They were laughing with relief. He followed on.

'And for once,' he cried cheerily, 'you don't need to worry about having a hangover in the morning – because there won't *be* any more mornings!'

He beamed at his happy, laughing audience. He glanced up at the sky, going through the same death routine every night, but his glance was only for a fraction of a second. He trusted it to do its job, as one professional trusts another.

'And now,' he said, strutting about the stage, 'at the risk of putting a damper on the wonderful sense of doom and futility here this evening, I would like to welcome a few parties.'

He pulled a card from his pocket.

'Do we have ...' He put up a hand to hold back the cheers. 'Do we have a party here from the Zansellquasure Flamarion Bridge Club from beyond the Vortvoid of Qvarne? Are they here?'

A rousing cheer came from the back, but he pretended not to hear. He peered around trying to find them.

'Are they here?' he asked again, to elicit a louder cheer.

He got it, as he always did.

'Ah, there they are. Well, last bids, lads – and no cheating, remember this is a very solemn moment.'

He lapped up the laughter.

'And do we also have, do we have ... a party of minor deities from the Halls of Asgard?'

Away to his right came a rumble of thunder. Lightning arced across the stage. A small group of hairy men with helmets sat looking very pleased with themselves, and raised their glasses to him.

Hasbeens, he thought to himself.

'Careful with the hammer, sir,' he said.

They did their trick with the lightning again. Max gave them a very thin-lipped smile.

'And thirdly,' he said, 'thirdly a party of Young Conservatives from Sirius B, are they here?'

A party of smartly dressed young dogs stopped throwing rolls at each other and started throwing rolls at the stage. They yapped and barked unintelligibly.

'Yes,' said Max, 'well, this is all your fault, you realize that?'

'And finally,' said Max, quieting the audience down and putting on his solemn face, 'finally I believe we have with us here tonight, a party of believers, very devout believers, from the Church of the Second Coming of the Great Prophet Zarquon.'

There were about twenty of them, sitting right out on

the edge of the floor, ascetically dressed, sipping mineral water nervously, and staying apart from the festivities. They blinked resentfully as the spotlight was turned on them.

'There they are,' said Max, 'sitting there, patiently. He said he'd come again, and he's kept you waiting a long time, so let's hope he's hurrying, fellas, because he's only got eight minutes left!'

The party of Xarquon's followers sat rigid, refusing to be buffeted by the waves of uncharitable laughter which swept over them.

Max restrained his audience.

'No, but seriously though folks, seriously, though, no offence meant. No, I know we shouldn't make fun of deeply held beliefs, so I think a big hand please for the Great Prophet Zarquon . . .'

The audience clapped respectfully.

'. . . wherever he's got to!'

He blew a kiss to the stony-faced party and returned to the centre of the stage.

He grabbed a tall stool and sat on it.

'It's marvellous, though,' he rattled on, 'to see so many of you here tonight – no isn't it, though? Yes, absolutely marvellous. Because I know that so many of you come here time and time again, which I think is really wonderful, to come and watch this final end of everything, and then return home to your own eras . . . and raise families, strive for new and better societies, fight terrible wars for what you know to be right . . . it really gives one hope for the future of all life-kind. Except, of course,' he waved at the blitzing turmoil above and around them, 'that we know it hasn't got one . . .'

Arthur turned to Ford – he hadn't quite got this place worked out in his mind.

'Look, surely,' he said, 'if the Universe is about to end . . . don't we go with it?'

Ford gave him a three-Pan-Galactic-Gargle-Blaster look, in other words a rather unsteady one.

'No,' he said. 'Look,' he said, 'as soon as you come into this dive you get held in this sort of amazing force-shielded temporal warp thing. I think.'

'Oh,' said Arthur. He turned his attention back to a bowl of soup he'd managed to get from the waiter to replace his steak.

'Look,' said Ford, 'I'll show you.'

He grabbed at a napkin off the table and fumbled hopelessly with it.

'Look,' he said again, 'imagine this napkin, right, as the temporal Universe, right? And this spoon as a transductional mode in the matter curve . . .'

It took him a while to say this last part, and Arthur hated to interrupt him.

'That's the spoon I was eating with,' he said.

'All right,' said Ford, 'imagine *this* spoon . . .' he found a small wooden spoon on a tray of relishes, 'this spoon . . .' but found it rather tricky to pick up, 'no, better still this fork . . .'

'Hey would you let go of my fork?' snapped Zaphod.

'All right,' said Ford, 'all right, all right. Why don't we say . . . why don't we say that this wine glass is the temporal Universe . . .'

'What, the one you've just knocked on the floor?'

'Did I do that?'

'Yes.'

'All right,' said Ford, 'forget that. I mean . . . I mean, look, do you know – do you know how the Universe actually began, for a kick off?'

'Probably not,' said Arthur, who wished he'd never embarked on any of this.

'All right,' said Ford, 'imagine this. Right You get this bath. Right. A large round bath. And it's made of ebony.'

'Where from?' said Arthur. 'Harrods was destroyed by the Vogons.'

'Doesn't matter.'

'So you keep saying.'

'Listen.'

'All right.'

'You get this bath, see? Imagine you've got this bath. And it's ebony. And it's conical.'

'Conical?' said Arthur. 'What sort of—'

'Shhh!' said Ford. 'It's conical. So what you do is, you see, you fill it with fine white sand, all right? Or sugar. Fine white sand, and/or sugar. Anything. Doesn't matter. Sugar's fine. And when it's full, you pull the plug out . . . are you listening?'

'I'm listening.'

'You pull the plug out, and it all just twirls away, twirls away you see, out of the plughole.'

'I see.'

'You don't see. You don't see at all. I haven't got to the clever bit yet. You want to hear the clever bit?'

'Tell me the clever bit.'

'I'll tell you the clever bit.'

Ford thought for a moment, trying to remember what the clever bit was.

'The clever bit,' he said, 'is this. You film it happening.'

'Clever,' agreed Arthur.

'You get a movie camera, and you film it happening.'

'Clever.'

'That's not the clever bit. This is the clever bit, I remember now that this is the clever bit. The clever bit is that you then thread the film in the projector . . . backwards!'

'Backwards?'

'Yes. Threading it backwards is definitely the clever bit. So then, you just sit and watch it, and everything just appears to spiral upwards out of the plughole and fill the bath. See?'

'And that's how the Universe began, is it?' said Arthur.

'No,' said Ford, 'but it's a marvellous way to relax.'

He reached for his wine glass.

'Where's my wine glass?' he said.

'It's on the floor.'

'Ah.'

Tipping back his chair to look for it, Ford collided with the small green waiter who was approaching the table carrying a portable telephone.

Ford excused himself to the waiter explaining that it was because he was extremely drunk.

The waiter said that that was quite all right and that he perfectly understood.

Ford thanked the waiter for his kind indulgence, attempted to tug his forelock, missed by six inches and slid under the table.

'Mr Zaphod Beeblebrox?' enquired the waiter.

'Er, yeah?' said Zaphod, glancing up from his third steak.

'There is a phone call for you.'

'Hey, what?'

'A phone call, sir.'

'For me? Here? Hey, but who knows where I am?'

One of his minds raced. The other dawdled lovingly over the food it was still shovelling in.

'Excuse me if I carry on, won't you?' said his eating head and carried on.

There were now so many people after him he'd lost count. He shouldn't have made such a conspicuous entrance. Hell, why not, though, he thought. How do you know you're having fun if there's no one watching you have it?

'Maybe somebody here tipped off the Galactic Police,' said Trillian. 'Everyone saw you come in.'

'You mean they want to arrest me over the phone?' said Zaphod. 'Could be. I'm a pretty dangerous dude when I'm cornered.'

'Yeah,' said a voice from under the table, 'you go to pieces so fast people get hit by the shrapnel.'

'Hey, what is this, Judgment Day?' snapped Zaphod.

'Do we get to see that as well?' asked Arthur nervously.

'I'm in no hurry,' muttered Zaphod. 'OK, so who's the cat on the phone?' He kicked Ford. 'Hey, get up there, kid,' he said to him, 'I may need you.'

'I am not,' said the waiter, 'personally acquainted with the metal gentleman in question, sir . . .'

'Metal?'

'Yes, sir.'

'Did you say metal?'

'Yes, sir. I said that I am not personally acquainted with the metal gentleman in question . . .'

'OK, carry on.'

'But I am informed that he has been awaiting your return for a considerable number of millennia. It seems you left here somewhat precipitately.'

'*Left* here?' said Zaphod. 'Are you being strange? We only just arrived here.'

'Indeed, sir,' persisted the waiter doggedly, 'but before you arrived here, sir, I understand that you left here.'

Zaphod tried this in one brain, then in the other.

'You're saying,' he said, 'that before we arrived here, we left here?'

This is going to be a long night, thought the waiter.

'Precisely, sir,' he said.

'Put your analyst on danger money, baby,' advised Zaphod.

'No, wait a minute,' said Ford, emerging above table level again, 'where exactly is here?'

'To be absolutely exact sir, it is Frogstar World B.'

'But we just *left* there,' protested Zaphod, 'we left there and came to the Restaurant at the End of the Universe.'

'Yes, sir,' said the waiter, feeling that he was now into the home stretch and running well, 'the one was constructed on the ruins of the other.'

'Oh,' said Arthur brightly, 'you mean we've travelled in time but not in space.'

'Listen, you semi-evolved simian,' cut in Zaphod, 'go climb a tree, will you?'

Arthur bristled.

'Go bang your heads together, four-eyes,' he advised Zaphod.

'No, no,' the waiter said to Zaphod, 'your monkey has got it right, sir.'

Arthur stuttered in fury and said nothing apposite, or indeed coherent.

'You jumped forward . . . I believe five hundred and seventy-six thousand million years whilst staying in exactly the same place,' explained the waiter. He smiled. He had a wonderful feeling that he had finally won through against what had seemed to be insuperable odds.

'That's it!' said Zaphod. 'I've got it. I told the computer to send us to the nearest place to eat, that's exactly what it did. Give or take five hundred and seventy-six thousand million years or whatever, we never moved. Neat.'

They all agreed this was very neat.

'But who,' said Zaphod, 'is the cat on the phone?'

'Whatever happened to Marvin?' said Trillian.

Zaphod clapped his hands to his heads.

'The Paranoid Android! I left him moping about on Frogstar B.'

'When was this?'

'Well, er, five hundred and seventy-six thousand million years ago, I suppose,' said Zaphod. 'Hey, er, hand me the rap-rod, Plate Captain.'

The little waiter's eyebrows wandered about his forehead in confusion.

'I beg your pardon, sir?' he said.

'The phone, waiter,' said Zaphod, grabbing it off him. 'Shee, you guys are so unhip it's a wonder your bums don't fall off.'

'Indeed, sir.'

'Hey, Marvin, is that you?' said Zaphod into the phone. 'How you doing, kid?'

There was a long pause before a thin low voice came up the line.

'I think you ought to know I'm feeling very depressed,' it said.

Zaphod cupped his hand over the phone.

'It's Marvin,' he said.

'Hey, Marvin,' he said into the phone again, 'we're having a great time. Food, wine, a little personal abuse and the Universe going foom. Where can we find you?'

Again the pause.

'You don't have to pretend to be interested in me, you know,' said Marvin at last. 'I know perfectly well I'm only a menial robot.'

'OK, OK,' said Zaphod, 'but where are you?'

'"Reverse primary thrust, Marvin," that's what they say to me, "Open airlock number three, Marvin. Marvin, can you pick up that piece of paper?" Can I pick up that piece of paper! Here I am, brain the size of a planet, and they ask me to . . .'

'Yeah, yeah,' sympathized Zaphod hardly at all.

'But I'm quite used to being humiliated,' droned Marvin, 'I can even go and stick my head in a bucket of water if you like. Would you like me to go and stick my head in a bucket of water? I've got one ready. Wait a minute.'

'Er, hey, Marvin . . .' interrupted Zaphod, but it was too late. Sad little clunks and gurgles came up the line.

'What's he saying?' asked Trillian.

'Nothing,' said Zaphod, 'he just phoned up to wash his head at us.'

'There,' said Marvin, coming back on the line and bubbling a bit, 'I hope that gave satisfaction . . .'

'Yeah, yeah,' said Zaphod, 'now will you please tell us where you are?'

'I'm in the car park,' said Marvin.

'The car park?' said Zaphod. 'What are you doing there?'

'Parking cars, what else does one do in a car park?'

'OK, hang in there, we'll be right down.'

In one movement Zaphod leapt to his feet, threw down the phone and wrote 'Hotblack Desiato' on the bill.

'Come on, guys,' he said, 'Marvin's in the car park. Let's get on down.'

'What's he doing in the car park?' asked Arthur.

'Parking cars, what else? Dum dum.'

'But what about the End of the Universe? We'll miss the big moment.'

'I've seen it. It's rubbish,' said Zaphod, 'nothing but a gnab gib.'

'A what?'

'Opposite of a big bang. Come on, let's get zappy.'

Few of the other diners paid them any attention as they weaved their way through the restaurant to the exit. Their eyes were riveted on the horror of the skies.

'An interesting effect to watch for,' Max was telling them, 'is in the upper left-hand quadrant of the sky, where if you look very carefully you can see the star system Hastromil boiling away into the ultra-violet. Anyone here from Hastromil?'

There were one or two slightly hesitant cheers from somewhere at the back.

'Well,' said Max beaming cheerfully at them, 'it's too late to worry about whether you left the gas on now.'

18

The main reception foyer was almost empty but Ford nevertheless weaved his way through it.

Zaphod grasped him firmly by the arm and manoeuvred him into a cubicle standing to one side of the entrance hall.

'What are you doing to him?' asked Arthur.

'Sobering him up,' said Zaphod and pushed a coin into a slot. Lights flashed, gases swirled.

'Hi,' said Ford stepping out a moment later, 'where are we going?'

'Down to the car park, come on.'

'What about the personnel Time Teleports?' said Ford. 'Get us straight back to the *Heart of Gold*.'

'Yeah, but I've cooled on that ship. Zarniwoop can have it. I don't want to play his games. Let's see what we can find.'

A Sirius Cybernetics Corporation Happy Vertical People Transporter took them down deep into the substrata beneath the Restaurant. They were glad to see it had been vandalized and didn't try to make them happy as well as take them down.

At the bottom of the shaft the lift doors opened and a blast of cold stale air hit them.

The first thing they saw on leaving the lift was a long concrete wall with over fifty doors in it offering lavatory facilities for all of fifty major lifeforms. Nevertheless, like every car park in the Galaxy throughout the entire history of car parks, this car park smelt predominantly of impatience.

They turned a corner and found themselves on a moving catwalk that traversed a vast cavernous space that stretched off into the dim distance.

It was divided off into bays each of which contained a space ship belonging to one of the diners upstairs, some smallish and utilitarian mass-production models, others vast shining limoships, the playthings of the very rich.

Zaphod's eyes sparkled with something that may or may not have been avarice as he passed over them. In fact it's best to be clear on this point – avarice is definitely what it was.

'There he is,' said Trillian. 'Marvin, down there.'

They looked where she was pointing. Dimly they could see a small metal figure listlessly rubbing a small rag on one remote corner of a giant silver suncruiser.

At short intervals along the moving catwalk, wide transparent tubes led down to floor level. Zaphod stepped off the catwalk into one of these and floated gently downwards. The others followed. Thinking back to this later, Arthur Dent thought it was the single most enjoyable experience of his travels in the Galaxy.

'Hey, Marvin,' said Zaphod striding over towards to him. 'Hey, kid, are we pleased to see you.'

Marvin turned, and in so far as it is possible for a totally inert metal face to look reproachful, this is what it did.

'No you're not,' he said, 'no one ever is.'

'Suit yourself,' said Zaphod and turned away to ogle the ships. Ford went with him.

Only Trillian and Arthur actually went up to Marvin.

'No, really we are,' said Trillian and patted him in a way that he disliked intensely, 'hanging around waiting for us all this time.'

'Five hundred and seventy-six thousand million, three thousand five hundred and seventy-nine years,' said Marvin. 'I counted them.'

'Well, here we are now,' said Trillian, feeling – quite correctly, in Marvin's view – that it was a slightly foolish thing to say.

'The first ten million years were the worst,' said Marvin, 'and the second ten million years, they were the worst too. The third ten million I didn't enjoy at all. After that I went into a bit of a decline.'

He paused just long enough to make them feel they ought to say something, and then interrupted.

'It's the people you meet in this job that really get you down,' he said and paused again.

Trillian cleared her throat.

'Is that—'

'The best conversation I had was over forty million years ago,' continued Marvin.

Again the pause.

'Oh d—'

'And that was with a coffee machine.'

He waited.

'That's a—'

'You don't like talking to me, do you?' said Marvin in a low desolate tone.

Trillian talked to Arthur instead.

Further down the chamber Ford Prefect had found something of which he very much liked the look, several such things in fact.

'Zaphod,' he said in a quiet voice, 'just look at some of these little star trolleys . . .'

Zaphod looked and liked.

The craft they were looking at was in fact pretty small but extraordinary, and very much a rich kid's toy. It was not much to look at. It resembled nothing so much as a paper dart about twenty feet long made of thin but tough metal foil. At the rear end was a small horizontal two-man cockpit. It had a tiny charm-drive engine, which was not capable of moving it at any great speed. The thing it did have, however, was a heat-sink.

The heat-sink had a mass of some two thousand billion tons and was contained within a black hole mounted in an electro-magnetic field situated halfway along the length of the ship, and this heat-sink enabled the craft to be manoeuvred to within a few miles of a yellow sun, there to catch and ride the solar flares that burst out from its surface.

Flare-riding is one of the most exotic and exhilarating sports in existence, and those who can dare and afford to do it are amongst the most lionized men in the Galaxy. It is also of course stupefyingly dangerous – those who don't die riding invariably die of sexual exhaustion at one of the Daedalus Club's Après-Flare parties.

Ford and Zaphod looked and passed on.

'And this baby,' said Ford, 'the tangerine star buggy with the black sunbusters . . .'

Again, the star buggy was a small ship – a totally misnamed one in fact, because the one thing it couldn't manage was interstellar distances. Basically it was a sporty planet hopper dolled up to look like something it wasn't. Nice lines, though. They passed on.

The next one was a big one and thirty yards long – a coach-built limoship and obviously designed with one aim in mind, that of making the beholder sick with envy. The paintwork and accessory detail clearly said 'Not only am I rich enough to afford this ship. I am also rich enough not to take it seriously'. It was wonderfully hideous.

'Just look at it,' said Zaphod, 'multi-cluster quark drive, perspulex running boards. Got to be a Lazlar Lyricon custom job.'

He examined every inch.

'Yes,' he said, 'look, the infra-pink lizard emblem on the neutrino cowling. Lazlar's trade mark. The man has no shame.'

'I was passed by one of these mothers once, out by the Axel Nebula,' said Ford. 'I was going flat out and this thing just strolled past me, star drive hardly ticking over. Just incredible.'

Zaphod whistled appreciatively.

'Ten seconds later,' said Ford, 'it smashed straight into the third moon of Jaglan Beta.'

'Yeah, right?'

'Amazing-looking ship, though. Looks like a fish, moves like a fish, steers like a cow.'

Ford looked round the other side.

'Hey, come see,' he called out. 'There's a big mural painted on this side. A bursting sun – Disaster Area's trade mark. This must be Hotblack's ship. Lucky old bugger. They do this terrible song, you know, which ends with a stuntship crashing into the sun. Meant to be an amazing spectacle. Expensive in stuntships, though.'

Zaphod's attention however was elsewhere. His attention was riveted on the ship standing next to Hotblack Desiato's limo. His mouths hung open.

'That,' he said, 'that . . . is really bad for the eyes . . .'

Ford looked. He too stood astonished.

It was a ship of classic, simple design, like a flattened salmon, twenty yards long, very clean, very sleek. There was just one remarkable thing about it.

'It's so ... *black*!' said Ford Prefect. 'You can hardly make out its shape ... light just seems to fall into it!'

Zaphod said nothing. He had simply fallen in love.

The blackness of it was so extreme that it was almost impossible to tell how close you were standing to it.

'Your eyes just slide off it ...' said Ford in wonder. It was an emotional moment. He bit his lip.

Zaphod moved forward to it, slowly, like a man possessed – or more accurately like a man who wanted to possess. His hand reached out to stroke it. His hand stopped. His hand reached out to stroke it again. His hand stopped again.

'Come and feel this surface,' he said in a hushed voice.

Ford put his hand out to feel it. His hand stopped.

'You ... you can't ...' he said.

'See?' said Zaphod. 'It's just totally frictionless. This must be one mother of a mover ...'

He turned to look at Ford seriously. At least, one of his heads did – the other stayed gazing in awe at the ship.

'What do you reckon, Ford?' he said.

'You mean ... er ...' Ford looked over his shoulder. 'You mean stroll off with it? You think we should?'

'No.'

'Nor do I.'

'But we're going to, aren't we.'

'How can we not?'

They gazed a little longer, till Zaphod suddenly pulled himself together.

'We better shift soon,' he said. 'In a moment or so the Universe will have ended and all the Captain Creeps will be pouring down here to find their bourge-mobiles.'

'Zaphod,' said Ford.

'Yeah?'

'How do we do it?'

'Simple,' said Zaphod. He turned. 'Marvin!' he called.

Slowly, laboriously, and with a million little clanking and creaking noises that he had learned to simulate, Marvin turned round to answer the summons.

'Come on over here,' said Zaphod. 'We've got a job for you.'

Marvin trudged towards them.

'I won't enjoy it,' he said.

'Yes you will,' enthused Zaphod, 'there's a whole new life stretching out ahead of you.'

'Oh, not another one,' groaned Marvin.

'Will you shut up and listen!' hissed Zaphod. 'This time there's going to be excitement and adventure and really wild things.'

'Sounds awful,' Marvin said.

'Marvin! All I'm trying to ask you . . .'

'I suppose you want me to open this spaceship for you?'

'What? Er . . . yes. Yeah, that's right,' said Zaphod jumpily. He was keeping at least three eyes on the entrance. Time was short.

'Well I wish you'd just tell me rather than try to engage my enthusiasm,' said Marvin, 'because I haven't got one.'

He walked on up to the ship, touched it, and a hatchway swung open.

Ford and Zaphod stared at the opening.

'Don't mention it,' said Marvin. 'Oh, you didn't.' He trudged away again.

Arthur and Trillian clustered round.

'What's happening?' asked Arthur.

'Look at this,' said Ford, 'look at the interior of this ship.'

'Weirder and weirder,' breathed Zaphod.

'It's black,' said Ford. 'Everything in it is just totally black . . .'

In the restaurant, things were fast approaching the moment after which there wouldn't be any more moments.

All eyes were fixed on the dome, other than those of Hotblack Desiato's bodyguard, which were looking intently at Hotblack Desiato, and those of Hotblack Desiato himself, which the bodyguard had closed out of respect.

The bodyguard leaned forward over the table. Had Hotblack Desiato been alive, he probably would have deemed this a good moment to lean back, or even go for a short walk. His bodyguard was not a man who improved with proximity. On account of his unfortunate condition, however, Hotblack Desiato remained totally inert.

'Mr Desiato, sir?' whispered the bodyguard. Whenever he spoke, it looked as if the muscles on either side of his mouth were clambering over each other to get out of the way.

'Mr Desiato? Can you hear me?'

Hotblack Desiato, quite naturally, said nothing.

'Hotblack?' hissed the bodyguard.

Again, quite naturally, Hotblack Desiato did not reply. Supernaturally, however, he did.

On the table in front of him a wine glass rattled, and a fork rose an inch or so and tapped against the glass. It settled on the table again.

The bodyguard gave a satisfied grunt.

'It's time we were going, Mr Desiato,' muttered the bodyguard, 'don't want to get caught in the rush, not in your condition. You want to get to the next gig nice and relaxed. There was a really big audience for it. One of the best. Kakrafoon. Five hundred and seventy-six thousand and two million years ago. Had you will have been looking forward to it?'

The fork rose again, paused, waggled in a non-committal sort of a way and dropped again.

'Ah, come on,' said the bodygyard, 'it's going to have been great. You knocked 'em cold.'The bodyguard would have given Dr Dan Streetmentioner an apoplectic attack.

'The black ship going into the sun always gets 'em, and the new one's a beauty. Be real sorry to see it go. If we get on down there, I'll set the black ship autopilot and we'll cruise off in the limo. OK?'

The fork tapped once in agreement, and the glass of wine mysteriously emptied itself.

The bodyguard wheeled Hotblack Desiato's chair out of the restaurant.

'And now,' cried Max from the centre of the stage, 'the moment you've all been waiting for!' He flung his arms into the air. Behind him, the band went into a frenzy of percussion and rolling synthochords. Max had argued with them about this but they had claimed it was in their contract that that's what they would do. His agent would have to sort it out.

'The skies begin to boil!' he cried. 'Nature collapses into the screaming void! In twenty seconds' time, the Universe itself will be at an end! See where the light of infinity bursts in upon us!'

The hideous fury of destruction blazed about them – and at that moment a still small trumpet sounded as from an infinite distance. Max's eyes swivelled round to glare at the band. None of them seemed to be playing a trumpet. Suddenly a wisp of smoke was swirling and shimmering on the stage next to him. The trumpet was joined by more trumpets. Over five hundred times Max had done this show, and nothing like this had ever happened before. He drew back in alarm from the swirling smoke, and as he did so, a figure slowly materialized inside, the figure of an ancient man, bearded, robed and wreathed in light. In his eyes were stars and on his brow a golden crown.

'What's this?' whispered Max, wild-eyed. 'What's happening?'

At the back of the restaurant the stony-faced party from the Church of the Second Coming of the Great Prophet Zarquon leapt ecstatically to their feet chanting and crying.

Max blinked in amazement. He threw up his arms to the audience.

'A big hand please, ladies and gentlemen,' he hollered, 'for the Great Prophet Zarquon! He has come! Zarquon has come again!'

Thunderous applause broke out as Max strode across the stage and handed his microphone to the Prophet.

Zarquon coughed. He peered round at the asembled gathering. The stars in his eyes twinkled uneasily. He handled the microphone with confusion.

'Er . . .' he said, 'hello. Er, look, I'm sorry I'm a bit late. I've had the most ghastly time, all sorts of things cropping up at the last moment.'

He seemed nervous of the expectant awed hush. He cleared his throat.

'Er, how are we for time?' he said. 'Have I just got a min—'

And so the Universe ended.

19

One of the major selling points of that wholly remarkable travel book, *The Hitchhiker's Guide to the Galaxy*, apart from its relative cheapness and the fact that it has the words DON'T PANIC written in large friendly letters on its cover, is its compendious and occasionally accurate glossary. The statistics relating to the geo-social nature of the Universe, for instance, are deftly set out between pages nine hundred and thirty-eight thousand three hundred and twenty-four and nine hundred and thirty-eight thousand three hundred and twenty-six; and the simplistic style in which they are written is partly explained by the fact that the editors, having to meet a publishing deadline, copied the information off the back of a packet of breakfast cereal, hastily embroidering it with a few footnotes in order to avoid prosecution under the incomprehensibly tortuous galactic copyright laws.

It is interesting to note that a later and wilier editor sent the book backwards in time through a temporal warp, and then successfully sued the breakfast cereal company for infringement of the same laws.

Here is a sample:

The Universe – some information to help you live in it.

1 **Area:** Infinite.
The Hitchhiker's Guide to the Galaxy *offers this definition of the word 'Infinite'.*
Infinite: *Bigger than the biggest thing ever and then some. Much bigger than that, in fact, really amazingly immense, a totally stunning size, real 'wow, that's big', time. Infinity is just so big that by comparison bigness itself looks really titchy. Gigantic multiplied by colossal multiplied by staggeringly huge is the sort of concept we're trying to get across here.*

2 **Imports:** None.
It is impossible to import things into an infinite area, there being no outside to import things in from.

3 **Exports:** None.
See Imports.

4 **Population:** None.
It is known that there are an infinite number of worlds, simply because there is an infinite amount of space for them to be in. However, not every one of them is inhabited. Therefore, there must be a finite number of inhabited worlds. Any finite number divided by infinity is as near to nothing as makes no odds, so the average population of all the planets in the Universe can be said to be zero. From this it follows that the population of the whole Universe is also zero, and that any people you may meet from time to time are merely the products of a deranged imagination.

5 **Monetary Units:** None.
In fact there are three freely convertible currencies in the Galaxy, but none of them count. The Altairian dollar has recently collapsed, the Flainian Pobble Bead is only exchangeable for other Flainian Pobble Beads, and the Triganic Pu has its own very special problems. Its exchange rate of eight Ningis to one Pu is simple enough, but since a Ningi is a triangular rubber coin six thousand eight hundred miles along each side, no one has ever collected enough to own one Pu. Ningis are not negotiable currency, because the Galactibanks refuse to deal in fiddling small change. From this basic premise it is very simple to prove that the Galactibanks are also the product of a deranged imagination.

6 **Art:** None.
The function of art is to hold the mirror up to nature, and there simply isn't a mirror big enough – see point one.

7 **Sex:** None.
Well, in fact there is an awful lot of this, largely

because of the total lack of money, trade, banks, art, or anything else that might keep all the non-existent people of the Universe occupied.

However, it is not worth embarking on a long discussion of it now because it really is terribly complicated. For further information see Guide *Chapters seven, nine, ten, eleven, fourteen, sixteen, seventeen, nineteen, twenty-one to eighty-four inclusive, and in fact most of the rest of the* Guide.

20

The restaurant continued existing, but everything else had stopped. Temporal relastatics held it and protected it in a nothingness that wasn't merely a vacuum, it was simply nothing – there was nothing in which a vacuum could be said to exist.

The force-shielded dome had once again been rendered opaque, the party was over, the diners were leaving, Zarquon had vanished along with the rest of the Universe, the Time Turbines were preparing to pull the restaurant back across the brink of time in readiness for the lunch sitting, and Max Quordlepleen was back in his small curtained dressing room trying to raise his agent on the tempophone.

In the car park stood the black ship, closed and silent.

In to the car park came the late Mr Hotblack Desiato, propelled along the moving catwalk by his bodyguard.

They descended one of the tubes. As they approached the limoship a hatchway swung down from its side, engaged the wheels of the wheelchair and drew it inside. The bodyguard followed, and having seen his boss safely connected up to his death-support system moved up to the small cockpit. Here he operated the remote control system which activated the autopilot in the black ship lying next to the limo, thus causing great relief to Zaphod Beeblebrox who had been trying to start the thing for over ten minutes.

The black ship glided smoothly forward out of its bay, turned, and moved down the central causeway swiftly and quietly. At the end it accelerated rapidly, flung itself into the temporal launch chamber and began the long journey back into the distant past.

The Milliways Lunch Menu quotes, by permission, a passage from *The Hitchhiker's Guide to the Galaxy*. The passage is this:

The history of every major galactic civilization tends to pass through three distinct and recognizable phases, those of Survival, Enquiry and Sophistication, otherwise known as the How, Why and Where phases.

For instance, the first phase is characterized by the question How can we eat?, the second by the question Why do we eat? and the third by the question Where shall we have lunch?

The Menu goes on to suggest that Milliways, the Restaurant at the End of the Universe, would be a very agreeable and sophisticated answer to that third question.

What it doesn't go on to say is that though it will usually take a large civilization many thousands of years to pass through the How, Why and Where phases, small social groupings under stressful conditions can pass through them with extreme rapidity.

'How are we doing?' said Arthur Dent.

'Badly,' said Ford Prefect.

'Where are we going?' said Trillian.

'I don't know,' said Zaphod Beeblebrox.

'Why not?' demanded Arthur Dent.

'Shut up,' suggested Zaphod Beeblebrox and Ford Prefect.

'Basically, what you're trying to say,' said Arthur Dent, ignoring this suggestion, 'is that we're out of control.'

The ship was rocking and swaying sickeningly as Ford and Zaphod tried to wrest control from the autopilot. The engines howled and whined like tired children in a supermarket.

'It's the wild colour scheme that freaks me,' said Zaphod whose love affair with this ship had lasted almost three minutes into the flight. 'Every time you try to operate one of these weird black controls that are labelled in black on a black background, a little black light lights up black to let you know you've done it. What is this? Some kind of galactic hyperhearse?'

The walls of the swaying cabin were also black, the ceiling was black, the seats – which were rudimentary since the only important trip this ship was designed for was supposed to be unmanned – were black, the control panel was black, the instruments were black, the little screws that held them in place were black, the thin tufted nylon floor covering was black, and when they had lifted up a corner of it they had discovered that the foam underlay also was black.

'Perhaps whoever designed it had eyes that responded to different wavelengths,' offered Trillian.

'Or didn't have much imagination,' muttered Arthur.

'Perhaps,' said Marvin, 'he was feeling very depressed.'

In fact, though they weren't to know it, the décor had been chosen in honour of its owner's sad, lamented and tax deductible condition.

The ship gave a particularly sickening lurch.

'Take it easy,' pleaded Arthur, 'you're making me space sick.'

'Time sick,' said Ford, 'we're plummeting backwards through time.'

'Thank you,' said Arthur, 'now I think I really am going to be ill.'

'Go ahead,' said Zaphod, 'we could do with a little colour about the place.'

'This is meant to be polite after-dinner conversation, is it?' snapped Arthur.

Zaphod left the controls to Ford to figure out, and lurched over to Arthur.

'Look, Earthman,' he said angrily, 'you've got a job to do, right? The Question to the Ultimate Answer, right?'

'What, that thing?' said Arthur. 'I thought we'd forgotten about that.'

'Not me, baby. Like the mice said, it's worth a lot of money in the right quarters. And it's all locked up in that head thing of yours.'

'Yes, but—'

'But nothing! Think about it. The Meaning of Life! We get our fingers on that, we can hold every shrink in the Galaxy up to ransom, and that's worth a bundle. I owe mine a mint.'

Arthur took a deep breath without much enthusiasm.

'All right,' he said, 'but where do we start? How should I know? They say the Ultimate Answer or whatever is Forty-two, how am I supposed to know what the question is? It could be anything. I mean, what's six times seven?'

Zaphod looked at him hard for a moment. Then his eyes blazed with excitement.

'Forty-two!' he cried.

Arthur wiped his palm across his forehead.

'Yes,' he said patiently, 'I know that.'

Zaphod's faces fell.

'I'm just saying the question could be anything at all,' said Arthur, 'and I don't see how I'm meant to know.'

'Because,' hissed Zaphod, 'you were there when your planet did the big firework.'

'We have a thing on Earth . . .' began Arthur.

'Had,' corrected Zaphod.

'. . . called tact. Oh never mind. Look, I just don't know.'

A low voice echoed dully round the cabin.

'I know,' said Marvin.

Ford called out from the controls he was still fighting a losing battle with.

'Stay out of this, Marvin,' he said, 'this is organism talk.'

'It's printed in the Earthman's brainwave patterns,' continued Marvin, 'but I don't suppose you'll be very interested in knowing that.'

'You mean,' said Arthur, 'you mean you can see into my mind?'

'Yes,' said Marvin.

Arthur stared in astonishment.

'And . . . ?' he said.

'It amazes me how you can manage to live in anything that small.'

'Ah,' said Arthur, 'abuse.'

'Yes,' confirmed Marvin.

'Ah, ignore him,' said Zaphod, 'he's only making it up.'

'Making it up?' said Marvin, swivelling his head in a parody of astonishment. 'Why should I want to make anything up? Life's bad enough as it is without wanting to invent any more of it.'

'Marvin,' said Trillian in the gentle, kindly voice that only she was still capable of assuming in talking to this misbegotten creature, 'if you knew all along, why then didn't you tell us?'

Marvin's head swivelled back to her.

'You didn't ask,' he said simply.

'Well, we're asking you now, metal man,' said Ford, turning round to look at him.

At that moment the ship suddenly stopped rocking and swaying, the engine pitch settled down to a gentle hum.

'Hey, Ford,' said Zaphod, 'that sounds good. Have you worked out the controls on this boat?'

'No,' said Ford, 'I just stopped fiddling with them. I reckon we just go to wherever this ship is going and get off it fast.'

'Yeah, right,' said Zaphod.

'I could tell you weren't really interested,' murmured Marvin to himself and slumped into a corner and switched himself off.

'Trouble is,' said Ford, 'that the one instrument in this whole ship that is giving any reading is worrying me. If it is what I think it is, and if it's saying what I think it's saying, then we've already gone too far back into the past. Maybe as much as two million years before our own time.'

Zaphod shrugged.

'Time is bunk,' he said.

'I wonder who this ship belongs to anyway,' said Arthur.

'Me,' said Zaphod.

'No. Who it really belongs to.'

'Really me,' insisted Zaphod, 'look, property is theft, right? Therefore theft is property. Therefore this ship is mine, OK?'

'Tell the ship that,' said Arthur.

Zaphod strode over to the console.

'Ship,' he said banging on the panels, 'this is your new owner speaking to . . .'

He got no further. Several things happened at once.

The ship dropped out of time travel mode and re-emerged into real space.

All the controls on the console, which had been shut down for the time trip, now lit up.

A large vision screen above the console winked into life revealing a wide starscape and a single very large sun dead ahead of them.

None of these things, however, was responsible for the fact that Zaphod was at the same moment hurled bodily backwards against the rear of the cabin, as were all the others.

They were hurled back by a single thunderous clap of noise that thudded out of the monitor speakers surrounding the vision screen.

21

Down on the dry, red world of Kakrafoon, in the middle of the vast Rudlit Desert, the stage technicians were testing the sound system.

That is to say, the sound system was in the desert, not the technicians. They had retreated to the safety of Disaster Area's giant control ship which hung in orbit some four hundred miles above the surface of the planet, and they were testing the sound from there. Anyone within five miles of the speaker silos wouldn't have survived the tuning up.

If Arthur Dent had been within five miles of the speaker silos then his expiring thought would have been that in both size and shape the sound rig closely resembled Manhattan. Risen out of the silos, the neutron-phase speaker stacks towered monstrously against the sky, obscuring the banks of plutonium reactors and seismic amps behind them.

Buried deep in concrete bunkers beneath the city of

speakers lay the instruments that the musicians would control from their ship, the massive photon-ajuitar, the base detonator and the Megabang drum complex.

It was going to be a noisy show.

Aboard the giant control ship, all was activity and bustle. Hotblack Desiato's limoship, a mere tadpole beside it, had arrived and docked, and the lamented gentleman was being transported down the high vaulted corridors to meet the medium who was going to interpret his psychic impulses on to the ajuitar keyboard.

A doctor, a logician and a marine biologist had also just arrived, flown in at phenomenal expense from Maximegalon to try to reason with the lead singer who had locked himself in the bathroom with a bottle of pills and was refusing to come out till it could be proved conclusively to him that he wasn't a fish. The bass player was busy machine-gunning his bedroom and the drummer was nowhere on board.

Frantic enquiries led to the discovery that he was standing on a beach on Santraginus V over a hundred light-years away where, he claimed, he had been happy for over half an hour now and had found a small stone that would be his friend.

The band's manager was profoundly relieved. It meant that for the seventeenth time on this tour the drums would be played by a robot and that therefore the timing of the cymballistics would be right.

The sub-etha was buzzing with the communications of the stage technicians testing the speaker channels, and this it was that was being relayed to the interior of the black ship.

Its dazed occupants lay against the back wall of the cabin, and listened to the voices on the monitor speakers.

'OK, channel nine on power,' said a voice, 'testing channel fifteen . . .'

Another thumping crack of noise walloped through the ship.

'Channel fifteen AOK,' said another voice.

A third voice cut in.

'The black stunt ship is now in position,' it said, 'it's looking good. Gonna be a great sundive. Stage computer on-line?'

A computer voice answered.

'On-line,' it said.

'Take control of the black ship.'

'Black ship locked into trajectory programme, on standby.'

'Testing channel twenty.'

Zaphod leaped across the cabin and switched frequencies on the sub-etha receiver before the next mind-pulverizing noise hit them. He stood there quivering.

'What,' said Trillian in a small quiet voice, 'does sundive mean?'

'It means,' said Marvin, 'that the ship is going to dive into the sun. Sun . . . Dive. It's very simple to understand. What do you expect if you steal Hotblack Desiato's stunt ship?'

'How do you know . . .' said Zaphod in a voice that would make a Vegan snow lizard feel chilly, 'that this is Hotblack Desiato's stuntship?'

'Simple,' said Marvin, 'I parked it for him.'

'Then why . . . didn't . . . you . . . tell us!'

'You said you wanted excitement and adventure and really wild things.'

'This is awful,' said Arthur unnecessarily in the pause which followed.

'That's what I said,' confirmed Marvin.

On a different frequency, the sub-etha receiver had

picked up a public broadcast, which now echoed round the cabin.

'... fine weather for the concert here this afternoon. I'm standing here in front of the stage,' the reporter lied, 'in the middle of the Rudlit Desert, and with the aid of hyperbinoptic glasses I can just about make out the huge audience cowering there on the horizon all around me. Behind me the speaker stacks rise like a sheer cliff face, and high above me the sun is shining away and doesn't know what's going to hit it. The environmentalist lobby do know what's going to hit it, and they claim that the concert will cause earthquakes, tidal waves, hurricanes, irreparable damage to the atmosphere, and all the usual things that environmentalists usually go on about.

'But I've just had a report that a representative of Disaster Area met with the environmentalists at lunchtime, and had them all shot, so nothing now lies in the way of—'

Zaphod switched it off. He turned to Ford.

'You know what I'm thinking?' he said.

'I think so,' said Ford.

'Tell me what you think I'm thinking.'

'I think you're thinking it's time we got off this ship.'

'I think you're right,' said Zaphod.

'I think you're right,' said Ford.

'How?' said Arthur.

'Quiet,' said Ford and Zaphod, 'we're thinking.'

'So this is it,' said Arthur, 'we're going to die.'

'I wish you'd stop saying that,' said Ford.

It is worth repeating at this point the theories that Ford had come up with, on his first encounter with human beings, to account for their peculiar habit of continually stating and restating the very very obvious, as in 'It's a nice day,' or 'You're very tall,' or 'So this is it, we're going to die.'

His first theory was that if human beings didn't keep exercising their lips, their mouths probably seized up.

After a few months of observation he had come up with a second theory, which was this – if human beings don't keep exercising their lips, their brains start working.

In fact, this second theory is more literally true of the Belcerebon people of Kakrafoon.

The Belcerebon people used to cause great resentment and insecurity amongst neighbouring races by being one of the most enlightened, accomplished, and above all quiet civilizations in the Galaxy.

As a punishment for this behaviour, which was held to be offensively self-righteous and provocative, a galactic tribunal inflicted on them that most cruel of all social diseases, telepathy. Consequently, in order to prevent themselves broadcasting every slightest thought that crosses their minds to anyone within a five-mile radius, they now have to talk very loudly and continuously about the weather, their little aches and pains, the match this afternoon and what a noisy place Kakrafoon has suddenly become.

Another method of temporarily blotting out their minds is to play host to a Disaster Area concert.

The timing of the concert was critical.

The ship had to begin its dive before the concert began in order to hit the sun six minutes and thirty-seven seconds before the climax of the song to which it related, so that the light of the solar flares had time to travel out to Kakrafoon.

The ship had already been diving for several minutes by the time that Ford Prefect had completed his search of the other compartments of the black ship. He burst back into the cabin.

The sun of Kakrafoon loomed terrifyingly large on the

vision screen, its blazing white inferno of fusing hydrogen nuclei growing moment by moment as the ship plunged onwards, unheeding the thumping and banging of Zaphod's hands on the control panel. Arthur and Trillian had the fixed expressions of rabbits on a night road who think that the best way of dealing with approaching headlights is to stare them out.

Zaphod span round, wild-eyed.

'Ford,' he said, 'how many escape capsules are there?'

'None,' said Ford.

Zaphod gibbered.

'Did you *count* them?' he yelled.

'Twice,' said Ford, 'did you manage to raise the stage crew on the radio?'

'Yeah,' said Zaphod bitterly, 'I said there were a whole bunch of people on board, and they said to say "hi" to everybody.'

Ford goggled.

'Didn't you tell them who you were?'

'Oh yeah. They said it was a great honour. That and something about a restaurant bill and my executors.'

Ford pushed Arthur aside roughly and leaned forward over the control console.

'Does *none* of this function?' he said savagely.

'All overridden.'

'Smash the autopilot.'

'Find it first. Nothing connects.'

There was a moment's cold silence.

Arthur was stumbling round the back of the cabin. He stopped suddenly.

'Incidentally,' he said, 'what does teleport mean?'

Another moment passed.

Slowly, the others turned to face him.

'Probably the wrong moment to ask,' said Arthur. 'It's just I remember hearing you use the word a short while ago and I only bring it up because . . .'

'Where,' said Ford Prefect quietly, 'does it say teleport?'

'Well, just over here, in fact,' said Arthur, pointing at a dark control box in the rear of the cabin. 'Just under the word "emergency", above the word "system" and beside the sign saying "out of order".'

In the pandemonium that instantly followed, the only action to follow was that of Ford Prefect lunging across the cabin to the small black box that Arthur had indicated and stabbing repeatedly at the single small black button set into it.

A six-foot square panel slid open beside it revealing a compartment which resembled a multiple shower unit that had found a new function in life as an electrician's junk store. Half-finished wiring hung from the ceiling, a jumble of abandoned components lay strewn on the floor, and the programming panel lolled out of the cavity in the wall into which it should have been secured.

A junior Disaster Area accountant, visiting the shipyard where this ship was being constructed, had demanded to know of the works foreman why the hell they were fitting an extremely expensive teleport into a ship which only had one important journey to make, and that unmanned. The foreman had explained that the teleport was available at a 10 per cent discount and the accountant had explained that this was immaterial; the foreman had explained that it was the finest, most powerful and sophisticated teleport that money could buy and the accountant had explained that the money did not wish to buy it; the foreman had explained that people would still need to enter and leave the ship and the accountant had explained that the ship sported a perfectly serviceable door; the foreman had explained that the accountant could go and boil his head and the accountant had explained to the foreman that the thing approaching him rapidly from his left was a knuckle sandwich. After the explanation had been concluded, work was discontinued on the teleport which subsequently passed unnoticed on the invoice as 'Sund. explns.' at five times the price.

'Hell's donkeys,' muttered Zaphod as he and Ford attempted to sort through the tangle of wiring.

After a moment or so Ford told him to stand back. He tossed a coin into the teleport and jiggled a switch on the lolling control panel. With a crackle and spit of light, the coin vanished.

'That much of it works,' said Ford, 'however, there is no guidance system. A matter transference teleport with no guidance programming could put you . . . well, anywhere.'

The sun of Kakrafoon loomed huge on the screen.

'Who cares,' said Zaphod, 'we go where we go.'

'And,' said Ford, 'there is no autosystem. We couldn't all go. Someone would have to stay and operate it.'

A solemn moment shuffled past. The sun loomed larger and larger.

'Hey, Marvin kid,' said Zaphod brightly, 'how you doing?'

'Very badly, I suspect,' muttered Marvin.

A shortish while later, the concert on Kakrafoon reached an unexpected climax.

The black ship with its single morose occupant had plunged on schedule into the nuclear furnace of the sun. Massive solar flares licked out from it millions of miles into space, thrilling and in a few cases spilling the dozen or so flare riders who had been coasting close to the surface of the sun in anticipation of the moment.

Moments before the flare light reached Kakrafoon the pounding desert cracked along a deep faultline. A huge and hitherto undetected underground river lying far beneath the surface gushed to the surface to be followed seconds later by the eruption of millions of tons of boiling lava that flowed hundreds of feet into the air, instantaneously vaporizing the river both above and below the surface in an explosion that echoed to the far side of the world and back again.

Those – very few – who witnessed the event and survived swear that the whole hundred thousand square miles of the desert rose into the air like a mile-thick pancake, flipped itself over and fell back down. At that precise moment the solar radiation from the flares filtered through the clouds of vaporized water and struck the ground.

A year later, the hundred thousand square mile desert was thick with flowers. The structure of the atmosphere around the planet was subtly altered. The sun blazed less harshly in the summer, the cold bit less bitterly in the winter, pleasant rain fell more often, and slowly the desert world of Kakrafoon became a paradise. Even the telepathic power with which the people of Kakrafoon had been cursed was permanently dispersed by the force of the explosion.

A spokesman for Disaster Area – the one who had had all the environmentalists shot – was later quoted as saying that it had been 'a good gig'.

Many people spoke movingly of the healing powers of music. A few sceptical scientists examined the records of the events more closely, and claimed that they had discovered faint vestiges of a vast artificially induced Improbability Field drifting in from a nearby region of space.

22

Arthur woke up and instantly regretted it. Hangovers he'd had, but never anything on this scale. This was it, this was the big one, this was the ultimate pits. Matter transference beams, he decided, were not as much fun as, say, a good solid kick in the head.

Being for the moment unwilling to move on account of a dull stomping throb he was experiencing, he lay a while and thought. The trouble with most forms of transport, he thought, is basically one of them not being worth all the bother. On Earth – when there had been an Earth, before it was demolished to make way for a new hyperspace bypass – the problem had been with cars. The disadvantages involved in pulling lots of black sticky slime from out of the ground where it had been safely hidden out of harm's way, turning it into tar to cover the land with, smoke to fill the air with and pouring the rest into the sea, all seemed to outweigh the advantages of being able to get more quickly from one place to another – particularly when the place you arrived at had probably become, as a result of this, very similar to the place you had left, i.e. covered with tar, full of smoke and short of fish.

And what about matter transference beams? Any form of transport which involved tearing you apart atom by atom, flinging those atoms through the sub-etha, and then jamming them back together again just when they were getting their first taste of freedom for years had to be bad news.

Many people had thought exactly this before Arthur Dent and had even gone to the lengths of writing songs about it. Here is one that used regularly to be chanted by huge crowds outside the Sirius Cybernetics Corporation Teleport Systems factory on Happi-Werld III:

Aldebaran's great, OK,
Algol's pretty neat,
Betelgeuse's pretty girls
Will knock you off your feet.
They'll do anything you like
Real fast and then real slow,
But if you have to take me apart to get me there
Then I don't want to go.

Singing,
Take me apart, take me apart,
What a way to roam,
And if you have to take me apart to get me there
I'd rather stay at home.

Sirius is paved with gold
So I've heard it said
By nuts who then go on to say
'See Tau before you're dead.'
I'll gladly take the high road
Or even take the low,
But if you have to take me apart to get me there
Then I, for one, won't go.

Singing,
Take me apart, take me apart,
You must be off your head,
And if you try to take me apart to get me there
I'll stay right here in bed.

. . . and so on. Another favourite song was much shorter:

I teleported home one night
With Ron and Sid and Meg.

Ron stole Meggie's heart away
And I got Sidney's leg.

Arthur felt the waves of pain slowly receding, though he was still aware of a dull stomping throb. Slowly, carefully, he stood up.

'Can you hear a dull stomping throb?' said Ford Prefect.

Arthur span round and wobbled uncertainly. Ford Prefect was approaching looking red-eyed and pasty.

'Where are we?' gasped Arthur.

Ford looked around. They were standing in a long curving corridor which stretched out of sight in both directions. The outer steel wall – which was painted in that sickly shade of pale green which they use in schools, hospitals and mental asylums to keep the inmates subdued – curved over the tops of their heads to where it met the inner perpendicular wall which, oddly enough was covered in dark brown hessian wall weave. The floor was of dark-green ribbed rubber.

Ford moved over to a very thick dark transparent panel set in the outer wall. It was several layers deep, yet through it he could see pinpoints of distant stars.

'I think we're in a spaceship of some kind,' he said.

Down the corridor came the sound of a dull stomping throb.

'Trillian?' called Arthur nervously. 'Zaphod?'

Ford shrugged.

'Nowhere about,' he said. 'I've looked. They could be anywhere. An unprogrammed teleport can throw you light-years in any direction. Judging by the way I feel I should think we've travelled a very long way indeed.'

'How do you feel?'

'Bad.'

'Do you think they're . . .'

'Where they are, how they are, there's no way we can't know and no way we can do anything about it. Do what I do.'

'What?'

'Don't think about it.'

Arthur turned this thought over in his mind, reluctantly saw the wisdom of it, tucked it up and put it away. He took a deep breath.

'Footsteps!' exclaimed Ford suddenly.

'Where?'

'That noise. That stomping throb. Pounding feet. Listen!'

Arthur listened. The noise echoed round the corridor at them from an indeterminate distance. It was the muffled sound of pounding footsteps, and it was noticeably louder.

'Let's move,' said Ford sharply. They both moved – in opposite directions.

'Not that way,' said Ford, 'that's where they're coming from.'

'No it's not,' said Arthur, 'they're coming from that way.'

'They're not, they're . . .'

They both stopped. They both turned. They both listened intently. They both agreed with each other. They both set off in opposite directions again.

Fear gripped them.

From both directions the noise was getting louder.

A few yards to their left another corridor ran at right angles to the inner wall. They ran to it and hurried along it. It was dark, immensely long and, as they passed down it, gave them the impression that it was getting colder and colder. Other corridors gave off it to the left and right, each very dark and each subjecting them to sharp blasts of icy air as they passed.

They stopped for a moment in alarm. The further

down the corridor they went, the louder became the sound of pounding feet.

They pressed themselves back against the cold wall and listened furiously. The cold, the dark and the drumming of disembodied feet was getting to them badly. Ford shivered, partly with cold, but partly with the memory of stories his favourite mother used to tell him when he was a mere slip of a Betelgeusian, ankle high to an Arcturan Megagrasshopper: stories of death ships, haunted hulks that roamed restlessly round the obscurer regions of deep space infested with demons or the ghosts of forgotten crews; stories too of incautious travellers who found and entered such ships; stories of . . . then Ford remembered the brown hessian wall weave in the first corridor and pulled himself together. However ghosts and demons may choose to decorate their death hulks, he thought to himself, he would lay any money you liked it wasn't with hessian wall weave. He grasped Arthur by the arm.

'Back the way we came,' he said firmly and they started to retrace their steps.

A moment later they leapt like startled lizards down the nearest corridor junction as the owners of the drumming feet suddenly hove into view directly in front of them.

Hidden behind the corner they goggled in amazement as about two dozen overweight men and women pounded past them in track suits panting and wheezing in a manner that would make a heart surgeon gibber.

Ford Prefect stared after them.

'Joggers!' he hissed, as the sound of their feet echoed away up and down the network of corridors.

'Joggers?' whispered Arthur Dent.

'Joggers,' said Ford Prefect with a shrug.

The corridor they were concealed in was not like the others. It was very short, and ended at a large steel door. Ford examined it, discovered the opening mechanism and pushed it wide.

The first thing that hit their eyes was what appeared to be a coffin.

And the next four thousand nine hundred and ninety-nine things that hit their eyes were also coffins.

23

The vault was low-ceilinged, dimly lit and gigantic. At the far end, about three hundred yards away an archway let through to what appeared to be a similar chamber, similarly occupied.

Ford Prefect let out a low whistle as he stepped down on to the floor of the vault.

'Wild,' he said.

'What's so great about dead people?' asked Arthur, nervously stepping down after him.

'Dunno,' said Ford. 'Let's find out, shall we?'

On closer inspection the coffins seemed to be more like sarcophagi. They stood about waist high and were constructed of what appeared to be white marble, which is almost certainly what it was – something that only appeared to be white marble. The tops were semi-translucent, and through them could dimly be perceived the features of their late and presumably lamented occupants. They were humanoid, and had clearly left the troubles of whatever world it was they came from far behind them, but beyond that little else could be discerned.

Rolling slowly round the floor between the sarcophagi was a heavy, oily white gas which Arthur at first thought might be there to give the place a little atmosphere until he discovered that it also froze his ankles. The sarcophagi too were intensely cold to the touch.

Ford suddenly crouched down beside one of them. He pulled a corner of his towel out of his satchel and started to rub furiously at something.

'Look, there's a plaque on this one,' he explained to Arthur, 'it's frosted over.'

He rubbed the frost clear and examined the engraved characters. To Arthur they looked like the footprints of a spider that had had one too many of whatever it is that spiders have on a night out, but Ford instantly recognized an early form of Galactic Eezzeereed.

'It says "Golgafrinchan Ark Fleet, Ship B, Hold Seven, Telephone Sanitizer Second Class" – and a serial number.'

'A telephone sanitizer?' said Arthur. 'A dead telephone sanitizer?'

'Best kind.'

'But what's he doing here?'

Ford peered through the top at the figure within.

'Not a lot,' he said, and suddenly flashed one of those grins of his which always made people think he'd been overdoing things recently and should try to get some rest.

He scampered over to another sarcophagus. A moment's brisk towel work and he announced:

'This one's a dead hairdresser. Hoopy!'

The next sarcophagus revealed itself to be the last resting place of an advertising account executive; the one after that contained a second-hand car salesman, third class.

An inspection hatch let into the floor suddenly caught Ford's attention, and he squatted down to unfasten it, thrashing away at the clouds of freezing gas that threatened to envelope him.

A thought occurred to Arthur.

'If these are just coffins,' he said, 'why are they kept so cold?'

'Or, indeed, why are they kept anyway?' said Ford tugging the hatchway open. The gas poured down through it. 'Why in fact is anyone going to all the trouble and expense of carting five thousand dead bodies through space?'

'Ten thousand,' said Arthur, pointing at the archway through which the next chamber was dimly visible.

Ford stuck his head down through the floor hatchway. He looked up again.

'Fifteen thousand,' he said. 'There's another lot down there.'

'Fifteen million,' said a voice.

'That's a lot,' said Ford. 'A lot a lot.'

'Turn around slowly,' barked the voice, 'and put your hands up. Any other move and I blast you into tiny tiny bits.'

'Hello?' said Ford, turning round slowly, putting his hands up and not making any other move.

'Why,' said Arthur Dent, 'isn't anyone ever pleased to see us?'

Standing silhouetted in the doorway through which they had entered the vault was the man who wasn't pleased to see them. His displeasure was communicated partly by the barking hectoring quality of his voice and partly by the viciousness with which he waved a long silver Kill-O-Zap gun at them. The designer of the gun had clearly not been instructed to beat about the bush. 'Make it evil,' he'd been told. 'Make it totally clear that this gun has a right end and a wrong end. Make it totally clear to anyone standing at the wrong end that things are going badly for them. If that means sticking all sorts of spikes and prongs and blackened bits all over it then so be it. This is not a gun for hanging over the fireplace or sticking in the umbrella stand, it is a gun for going out and making people miserable with.'

Ford and Arthur looked at the gun unhappily.

The man with the gun moved from the door and circled round them. As he came into the light they could see his black and gold uniform on which the buttons were so highly polished that they shone with an intensity that would have made an approaching motorist flash his lights in annoyance.

He gestured at the door.

'Out,' he said. People who can supply that amount of fire power don't need to supply verbs as well. Ford and Arthur went out, closely followed by the wrong end of the Kill-O-Zap gun and the buttons.

Turning into the corridor they were jostled by twenty-four oncoming joggers, now showered and changed, who swept on past them into the vault. Arthur turned to watch them in confusion.

'Move!' screamed their captor.

Arthur moved.

Ford shrugged and moved.

In the vault the joggers went to twenty-four empty sarcophagi along the side wall, opened them, climbed in, and fell into twenty-four dreamless sleeps.

24

'Er, Captain . . .'

'Yes, Number One?'

'Just had a sort of report thingy from Number Two.'

'Oh dear.'

High up in the bridge of the ship, the captain stared out into the infinite reaches of space with mild irritation.

From where he reclined beneath a wide domed bubble he could see before and above him the vast panorama of stars through which they were moving – a panorama that had thinned out noticably during the course of the voyage. Turning and looking backwards, over the vast two-mile bulk of the ship, he could see the far denser mass of stars behind them which seemed to form almost a solid band. This was the view through the galactic centre from which they were travelling, and indeed had been travelling for years, at a speed that he couldn't quite remember at the moment, but he knew it was terribly fast. It was something approaching the speed of something or other, or was it three times the speed of something else? Jolly impressive, anyway. He peered into the bright distance behind the ship, looking for something. He did this every few minutes or so, but never found what he was looking for. He didn't let it worry him, though. The scientist chaps had been very insistent that everything was going to be perfectly all right providing nobody panicked and everybody got on and did their bit in an orderly fashion.

He wasn't panicking. As far as he was concerned everything was going splendidly. He dabbed at his shoulder with a large frothy sponge. It crept back into his mind that he was feeling mildly irritated about something. Now what was all that about? A slight cough alerted him to the fact that the ship's first officer was still standing nearby.

Nice chap, Number One. Not of the very brightest, had the odd spot of difficulty doing up his shoe laces, but jolly good officer material for all that. The captain wasn't a man to kick a chap when he was bending over trying to do up his shoe laces, however long it took him. Not like that ghastly Number Two, strutting about all over the place, polishing his buttons, issuing reports every hour; 'Ship's still moving, Captain.' 'Still on course, Captain.' 'Oxygen levels still being maintained, Captain.' 'Give it a miss,' was the captain's vote. Ah yes, that was the thing that had been irritating him. He peered down at Number One.

'Yes, Captain, he was shouting something or other about having found some prisoners . . .'

The captain thought about this. Seemed pretty unlikely to him, but he wasn't one to stand in his officers' way.

'Well, perhaps that'll keep him happy for a bit,' he said, 'he's always wanted some.'

Ford Prefect and Arthur Dent trudged onwards up the ship's apparently endless corridors. Number Two marched behind them barking the occasional order about not making any false moves or trying any funny stuff. They seemed to have passed at least a mile of continuous brown hessian wall weave. Finally they reached a large steel door which slid open when Number Two shouted at it.

They entered.

To the eyes of Ford Prefect and Arthur Dent, the most remarkable thing about the ship's bridge was not the fity-foot diameter hemispherical dome which covered it, and through which the dazzling display of stars shone down on them: to people who have eaten at the Restaurant at the End of the Universe, such wonders are commonplace. Nor was it the bewildering array of instruments that crowded the long circumferential wall around them. To Arthur this was exactly what spaceships were traditionally supposed to look like, and to Ford it looked thoroughly antiquated: it confirmed his supicions that Disaster Area's stuntship had taken them back at least a million, if not two million, years before their own time.

No, the thing that really caught them off balance was the bath.

The bath stood on a six-foot pedestal of rough-hewn blue water crystal and was of a baroque monstrosity not often seen outside the Maximegalon Museum of Diseased Imaginings. An intestinal jumble of plumbing had been picked out in gold leaf rather than decently buried at midnight in an unmarked grave; the taps and shower attachment would have made a gargoyle jump.

As the dominant centrepiece of a starship bridge it was terribly wrong, and it was with the embittered air of a man who knew this that Number Two approached it.

'Captain, sir!' he shouted through clenched teeth – a difficult trick but he'd had years during which to perfect it.

A large genial face and a genial foam-covered arm popped up above the rim of the monstrous bath.

'Ah, hello, Number Two,' said the captain, waving a cheery sponge, 'having a nice day?'

Number Two snapped even further to attention than he already was.

'I have brought you the prisoners I located in freezer bay seven, sir!' he yapped.

Ford and Arthur coughed in confusion.

'Er . . . hello,' they said.

The captain beamed at them. So Number Two had really found some prisoners. Well, good for him, thought the captain, nice to see a chap doing what he's best at.

'Oh, hello there,' he said to them. 'Excuse me not getting up, just having a quick bath. Well, jynnan tonnyx all round, then. Look in the fridge, Number One.'

'Certainly, sir.'

It is a curious fact, and one to which no one knows

quite how much importance to attach, that something like 85 per cent of all known worlds in the Galaxy, be they primitive or highly advanced, have invented a drink called jynnan tonnyx, or gee-N'N-T'N-ix, or jinond-o-nicks, or any one of a thousand or more variations on the same phonetic theme. The drinks themselves are not the same, and vary between the Sivolvian 'chinanto/mnigs', which is ordinary water served at slightly above room temperature, and the Gagrakackan 'tzjin-anthony-ks' which kills cows at a hundred paces; and in fact the one common factor between all of them, beyond the fact that the names sound the same, is that they were all invented and named *before* the worlds concerned made contact with any other worlds.

What can be made of this fact? It exists in total isolation. As far as any theory of structural linguistics is concerned it is right off the graph, and yet it persists. Old structural linguists get very angry when young structural linguists go on about it. Young structural linguists get deeply excited about it and stay up late at night convinced that they are very close to something of profound importance, and end up becoming old structural linguists before their time, getting very angry with the young ones. Structural linguistics is a bitterly divided and unhappy discipline, and a large number of its practitioners spend too many nights drowning their problems in ouisghian zodahs.

Number Two stood before the captain's bathtub trembling with frustration.

'Don't you want to interrogate the prisoners, sir?' he squealed.

The captain peered at him in bemusement.

'Why on Golgafrinchan should I want to do that?' he asked.

'To get information out of them, sir! To find out why they came here!'

'Oh no, no, no,' said the captain, 'I expect they just dropped in for a quick jynnan tonnyx, don't you?'

'But sir, they're my prisoners! I must interrogate them!'

The captain looked at them doubtfully.

'Oh all right,' he said, 'if you must. Ask them what they want to drink.'

A hard cold gleam came into Number Two's eyes. He advanced slowly on Ford Prefect and Arthur Dent.

'All right, you scum,' he growled, 'you vermin . . .' He jabbed Ford with the Kill-O-Zap gun.

'Steady on, Number Two,' admonished the captain gently.

'What do you want to drink!!!' Number Two screamed.

'Well, the jynnan tonnyx sounds very nice to me,' said Ford. 'What about you, Arthur?'

Arthur blinked.

'What? Oh, er, yes,' he said.

'With ice or without?' bellowed Number Two.

'Oh, with, please,' said Ford.

'Lemon??!!'

'Yes, please,' said Ford, 'and do you have any of those little biscuits? You know, the cheesy ones?'

'I'm asking the questions!!!!' howled Number Two, his body quaking with apoplectic fury.

'Er, Number Two . . .' said the captain softly.

'Sir?!'

'Push off, would you, there's a good chap. I'm trying to have a relaxing bath.'

Number Two's eyes narrowed and became what are known in the Shouting and Killing People trade as cold slits, the idea presumably being to give your opponent the impression that you have lost your glasses or are having difficulty keeping awake. Why this is frightening is an, as yet, unresolved problem.

He advanced on the captain, his (Number Two's)

mouth a thin hard line. Again, tricky to know why this is understood as fighting behaviour. If, whilst wandering through the jungle of Traal, you were suddenly to come upon the fabled Ravenous Bugblatter Beast, you would have reason to be grateful if its mouth was a thin hard line rather than, as it usually is, a gaping mass of slavering fangs.

'May I remind you, sir,' hissed Number Two at the captain, 'that you have now been in that bath for over *three years*?!' This final shot delivered, Number Two spun on his heel and stalked off to a corner to practise darting eye movements in the mirror.

The captain squirmed in his bath. He gave Ford Prefect a lame smile.

'Well, you need to relax a lot in a job like mine,' he said.

Ford slowly lowered his hands. It provoked no reaction. Arthur lowered his.

Treading very slowly and carefully, Ford moved over to the bath pedestal. He patted it.

'Nice,' he lied.

He wondered if it was safe to grin. Very slowly and carefully, he grinned. It was safe.

'Er . . .' he said to the captain.

'Yes?' said the captain.

'I wonder,' said Ford, 'could I ask you actually what your job is, in fact?'

A hand tapped him on the shoulder. He span round.

It was the first officer.

'Your drinks,' he said.

'Ah, thank you,' said Ford. He and Arthur took their jynnan tonnyx. Arthur sipped his, and was surprised to discover it tasted very like a whisky and soda.

'I mean, I couldn't help noticing,' said Ford, also taking a sip, 'the bodies. In the hold.'

'Bodies?' said the captain in surprise.

Ford paused and thought to himself. Never take anything for granted, he thought. Could it be that the captain doesn't know he's got fifteen million dead bodies on his ship?

The captain was nodding cheerfully at him. He also appeared to be playing with a rubber duck.

Ford looked around. Number Two was staring at him in the mirror, but only for an instant: his eyes were constantly on the move. The first officer was just standing there holding the drinks tray and smiling benignly.

'Bodies?' said the captain again.

Ford licked his lips.

'Yes,' he said. 'All those dead telephone sanitizers and account executives, you know, down in the hold.'

The captain stared at him. Suddenly he threw back his head and laughed.

'Oh they're not dead,' he said. 'Good Lord, no, no they're frozen. They're going to be revived.'

Ford did something he very rarely did. He blinked.

Arthur seemed to come out of a trance.

'You mean you've got a hold full of frozen hairdressers?' he said.

'Oh yes,' said the captain, 'millions of them. Hairdressers, tired TV producers, insurance salesmen, personnel officers, security guards, public relations executives, management consultants, you name it. We're going to colonize another planet.'

Ford wobbled very slightly.

'Exciting, isn't it?' said the captain.

'What, with that lot?' said Arthur.

'Ah, now don't misunderstand me,' said the captain, 'we're just one of the ships in the Ark Fleet. We're the "B" Ark you see. Sorry, could I just ask you to run a bit more hot water for me?'

Arthur obliged, and a cascade of pink frothy water

swirled around the bath. The captain let out a sigh of pleasure.

'Thank you so much, my dear fellow. Do help yourselves to more drinks, of course.'

Ford tossed down his drink, took the bottle from the first officer's tray and refilled his glass to the top.

'What,' he said, 'is a "B" Ark?'

'This is,' said the captain, and swished the foamy water around joyfully with the duck.

'Yes,' said Ford, 'but . . .'

'Well, what happened you see was,' said the captain, 'our planet, the world from which we have come, was, so to speak, doomed.'

'Doomed?'

'Oh yes. So what everyone thought was, let's pack the whole population into some giant spaceships and go and settle on another planet.'

Having told this much of his story, he settled back with a satisfied grunt.

'You mean a less doomed one?' prompted Arthur.

'What did you say, dear fellow?'

'A less doomed planet. You were going to settle on.'

'Are going to settle on, yes. So it was decided to build three ships, you see, three Arks in space, and . . . I'm not boring you, am I?'

'No, no,' said Ford firmly, 'it's fascinating.'

'You know it's delightful,' reflected the captain, 'to have someone else to talk to for a change.'

Number Two's eyes darted feverishly about the room again and then settled back on the mirror, like a pair of flies briefly distracted from their favourite piece of month-old meat.

'Trouble with a long journey like this,' continued the captain, 'is that you end up just talking to yourself a lot, which gets terribly boring because half the time you know what you're going to say next.'

'Only half the time?' asked Arthur in surprise.

The captain thought for a moment.

'Yes, about half I'd say. Anyway – where's the soap?' He fished around and found it.

'Yes, so anyway,' he resumed, 'the idea was that into the first ship, the "A" ship, would go all the brilliant leaders, the scientists, the great artists, you know, all the achievers; and then into the third, or "C" ship, would go all the people who did the actual work, who made things and did things; and then into the "B" ship – that's us – would go everyone else, the middlemen, you see.'

He smiled happily at them.

'And we were sent off first,' he concluded, and hummed a little bathing tune.

The little bathing tune, which had been composed for him by one of his world's most exciting and prolific jingle writers (who was currently asleep in hold thirty-six some nine hundred yards behind them) covered what would otherwise have been an awkward moment of silence. Ford and Arthur shuffled their feet and furiously avoided each other's eyes.

'Er . . .' said Arthur after a moment, 'what exactly was it that was wrong with your planet, then?'

'Oh, it was doomed, as I said,' said the captain. 'Apparently it was going to crash into the sun or something. Or maybe it was that the moon was going to crash into us. Something of the kind. Absolutely terrifying prospect whatever it was.'

'Oh,' said the first officer suddenly, 'I thought it was that the planet was going to be invaded by a gigantic swarm of twelve-foot piranha bees. Wasn't that it?'

Number Two span around, eyes ablaze with a cold hard light that only comes with the amount of practice he was prepared to put in.

'That's not what I was told!' he hissed. 'My commanding officer told me that the entire planet was in imminent danger of being eaten by an enormous mutant star goat!'

'Oh really . . .' said Ford Prefect.

'Yes! A monstrous creature from the pit of hell with scything teeth ten thousand miles long, breath that would boil oceans, claws that could tear continents from their roots, a thousand eyes that burned like the sun, slavering jaws a million miles across, a monster such as you have never . . . never . . . ever . . .'

'And they made sure they sent your lot off first, did they?' enquired Arthur.

'Oh yes,' said the captain, 'well, everyone said, very nicely, I thought, that it was very important for morale to feel that they would be arriving on a planet where they could be sure of a good haircut and where the phones were clean.'

'Oh yes,' agreed Ford, 'I can see that would be very important. And the other ships, er . . . they followed on after you, did they?'

For a moment the captain did not answer. He twisted round in his bath and gazed backwards over the huge bulk of the ship towards the bright galactic centre. He squinted into the inconceivable distance.

'Ah. Well it's funny you should say that,' he said and allowed himself a slight frown at Ford Prefect, 'because curiously enough we haven't heard a peep out of them since we left five years ago . . . but they must be behind us somewhere.'

He peered off into the distance again.

Ford peered with him and gave a thoughtful frown.

'Unless, of course,' he said softly, 'they were eaten by the goat . . .'

'Ah yes . . .' said the captain, with a slight hesitancy creeping into his voice, 'the goat . . .' His eyes passed over the solid shapes of the instruments and computers that lined the bridge. They winked away innocently at him. He stared out at the stars, but none of them said a word. He glanced at his first and second officers, but they seemed lost in their own thoughts for a moment. He glanced at Ford Prefect, who raised his eyebrows at him.

'It's a funny thing, you know,' said the captain at last, 'but now that I actually come to tell the story to someone else . . . I mean does it strike you as odd, Number One?'

'Errrrrrrrrrr . . .' said Number One.

'Well,' said Ford, 'I can see that you've got a lot of things you're going to want to talk about, so, thanks for the drinks, and if you could sort of drop us off at the nearest convenient planet . . .'

'Ah, well that's a little difficult, you see,' said the captain, 'because our trajectory thingy was preset before we left Golgafrinchan, I think partly because I'm not very good with figures . . .'

'You mean we're stuck here on this ship?' exclaimed Ford suddenly losing patience with the whole charade. 'When are you meant to be reaching this planet you're meant to be colonizing?'

'Oh, we're nearly there, I think,' said the captain, 'any second now. It's probably time I was getting out of this bath, in fact. Oh, I don't know though, why stop just when I'm enjoying it?'

'So we're actually going to land in a minute?' said Arthur.

'Well not so much *land*, in fact, not actually land as such, no . . . er . . .'

'What are you talking about?' asked Ford sharply.

'Well,' said the captain, picking his way through the words carefully, 'I think as far as I can remember we were programmed to crash on it.'

'Crash?' shouted Ford and Arthur.

'Er, yes,' said the captain, 'yes, it's all part of the plan, I think. There was a terribly good reason for it which I can't quite remember at the moment. It was something to do with . . . er . . .'

Ford exploded.

'You're a load of useless bloodly loonies!' he shouted.

'Ah yes, that was it,' beamed the captain, 'that was the reason.'

25

The Hitchhiker's Guide to the Galaxy, has this to say about the planet of Golgafrinchan: *it is a planet with an ancient and mysterious history, rich in legend, red, and occasionally green, with the blood of those who sought in times gone by to conquer her; a land of parched and barren landscapes, of sweet and sultry air heady with the scent of the perfumed springs that trickle over its hot and dusty rocks and nourish the dark and musky lichens beneath; a land of fevered brows and intoxicated imaginings, particularly amongst those who taste the lichens; a land also of cool and shaded thoughts amongst those who have learnt to forswear the lichens and find a tree to sit beneath; a land also of steel and blood and heroism; a land of the body and of the spirit. This was its history.*

And in all this ancient and mysterious history, the most mysterious figures of all were without doubt those of the Great Circling Poets of Arium. These Circling Poets used to live in remote mountain passes where they would lie in wait for small bands of unwary travellers, circle round them, and throw rocks at them.

And when the travellers cried out, saying why didn't they go away and get on with writing some poems instead of pestering people with all this rock-throwing business, they would suddenly stop, and then break into one of the seven hundred and ninety-four great Song Cycles of Vassillian.

These songs were all of extraordinary beauty, and even more extraordinary length, and all fell into exactly the same pattern.

The first part of each song would tell how there once went forth from the city of Vassillian a party of five sage princes and four horses. The princes, who are of course brave, noble and wise, travel widely in distant lands, fight giant ogres, pursue exotic philosophies, take tea with weird gods and rescue beautiful monsters from ravening princesses before finally announcing that they have achieved enlightenment and that their wanderings are therefore accomplished.

The second, and much longer, part of each song would then tell of all their bickerings about which one of them is going to have to walk back.

All this lay in the planet's remote past. It was, however, a descendant of one of these eccentric poets who invented the spurious tales of impending doom which enabled the people of Golgafrinchan to rid themselves of an entire useless third of their population. The other two-thirds stayed firmly at home and lived full, rich and happy lives until they were all suddenly wiped out by a virulent disease contracted from a dirty telephone.

26

That night the ship crash-landed on an utterly insignificant little blue-green planet which circled a small unregarded yellow sun in the uncharted backwaters of the unfashionable end of the Western Spiral Arm of the Galaxy.

In the hours preceding the crash Ford Prefect had fought furiously but in vain to unlock the controls of the ship from their pre-ordained flight path. It had quickly become apparent to him that the ship had been programmed to convey its pay-load safely, if uncomfortably, to its new home but to cripple itself beyond all hope of repair in the process.

Its screaming, blazing descent through the atmosphere had stripped away most of its superstructure and outer shielding, and its final inglorious bellyflop into a murky swamp had left its crew only a few hours of darkness during which to revive and offload its deep-frozen and unwanted cargo, for the ship began to settle almost at once, slowly upending its gigantic bulk in the stagnant slime. Once or twice during the night it was starkly silhouetted against the sky as burning meteors – the detritus of its descent – flashed across the sky.

In the grey pre-dawn light it let out an obscene roaring gurgle and sank for ever into the stinking depths.

When the sun came up that morning it shed its thin watery light over a vast area heaving with wailing hairdressers, public-relations executives, opinion pollsters and the rest, all clawing their way desperately to dry land.

A less strong-minded sun would probably have gone straight back down again, but it continued to climb its way through the sky and after a while the influence of its warming rays began to have some restoring effect on the feebly struggling creatures.

Countless numbers had, unsurprisingly, been lost to the swamp in the night, and millions more had been sucked down with the ship, but those that survived still numbered hundreds of thousands and as the day wore on they crawled out over the surrounding countryside, each looking for a few square feet of solid ground on which to collapse and recover from their nightmare ordeal.

*

Two figures moved further afield.

From a nearby hillside Ford Prefect and Arthur Dent watched the horror of which they could not feel a part.

'Filthy dirty trick to pull,' muttered Arthur.

Ford scraped a stick along the ground and shrugged.

'An imaginative solution to a problem, I'd have thought,' he said.

'Why can't people just learn to live together in peace and harmony?' said Arthur.

Ford gave a loud, very hollow laugh.

'Forty-two!' he said with a malicious grin. 'No, doesn't work. Never mind.'

Arthur looked at him as if he'd gone mad and, seeing nothing to indicate to the contrary, realized that it would be perfectly reasonable to assume that this had in fact happened.

'What do you think will happen to them all?' he said after a while.

'In an infinite Universe anything can happen,' said Ford, 'Even survival. Strange but true.'

A curious look came into his eyes as they passed over the landscape and then settled again on the scene of misery below them.

'I think they'll manage for a while,' he said.

Arthur looked up sharply.

'Why do you say that?' he said.

Ford shrugged.

'Just a hunch,' he said, and refused to be drawn on any further questions.

'Look,' he said suddenly.

Arthur followed his pointing finger. Down amongst the sprawling masses a figure was moving – or perhaps lurching would be a more accurate description. He appeared to be carrying something on his shoulder. As he lurched from prostrate form to prostrate form he seemed to wave whatever the something was at them in a drunken fashion. After a while he gave up the struggle and collapsed in a heap.

Arthur had no idea what this was meant to mean to him.

'Movie camera,' said Ford. 'Recording the historic moment.'

'Well, I don't know about you,' said Ford again after a moment, 'but I'm off.'

He sat a while in silence.

After a while this seemed to require comment.

'Er, when you say you're off, what do you mean exactly?' said Arthur.

'Good question,' said Ford, 'I'm getting total silence.'

Looking over his shoulder Arthur saw that he was twiddling with knobs on a small black box. Ford had already introduced this box to Arthur as a Sub-Etha Sens-O-Matic, but Arthur had merely nodded absently and not pursued the matter. In his mind the Universe still divided into two parts – the Earth, and everything else. The Earth having been demolished to make way for a hyperspace bypass meant that this view of things was a little lopsided, but Arthur tended to cling to that lopsidedness as being his last remaining contact with his home. Sub-Etha Sens-O-Matics belonged firmly in the 'everything else' category.

'Not a sausage,' said Ford, shaking the thing.

Sausage, thought Arthur to himself as he gazed listlessly at the primitive world about him, what I wouldn't give for a good Earth sausage.

'Would you believe,' said Ford in exasperation, 'that there are no transmissions of any kind within light-years of this benighted tip? Are you listening to me?'

'What?' said Arthur.

'We're in trouble,' said Ford.

'Oh,' said Arthur. This sounded like month-old news to him.

'Until we pick up anything on this machine,' said Ford, 'our chances of getting off this planet are zero. It may be some freak standing wave effect in the planet's magnetic field – in which case we just travel round and round till we find a clear reception area. Coming?'

He picked up his gear and strode off.

Arthur looked down the hill. The man with the movie camera had struggled back up to his feet just in time to film one of his colleagues collapsing.

Arthur picked a blade of grass and strode off after Ford.

27

'I trust you had a pleasant meal?' said Zarniwoop to Zaphod and Trillian as they rematerialized on the bridge of the starship *Heart of Gold* and lay panting on the floor.

Zaphod opened some eyes and glowered at him.

'You,' he spat. He staggered to his feet and stomped off to find a chair to slump into. He found one and slumped into it.

'I have programmed the computer with the Improbability Coordinates pertinent to our journey,' said Zarniwoop, 'we will arrive there very shortly. Meanwhile, why don't you relax and prepare yourself for the meeting?'

Zaphod said nothing. He got up again and marched over to a small cabinet from which he pulled a bottle of Old Janx Spirit. He took a long pull at it.

'And when this is all done,' said Zaphod savagely, 'it's done, all right? I'm free to go and do what the hell I like and lie on beaches and stuff?'

'It depends what transpires from the meeting,' said Zarniwoop.

'Zaphod, who is this man?' said Trillian shakily, wobbling to her feet. 'What's he doing here? Why's he on our ship?'

'He's a very stupid man,' said Zaphod, 'who wants to meet the man who rules the Universe.'

'Ah,' said Trillian taking the bottle from Zaphod and helping herself, 'a social climber.'

28

The major problem – *one* of the major problems, for there are several – one of the many major problems with governing people is that of who you get to do it; or rather of who manages to get people to let them do it to them.

To summarize: it is a well-known fact, that those people who most *want* to rule people are, ipso facto, those least suited to do it. To summarize the summary: anyone who is capable of getting themselves made President should on no account be allowed to do the job. To summarize the summary of the summary: people are a problem.

And so this is the situation we find: a succession of Galactic Presidents who so much enjoy the fun and palaver of being in power that they very rarely notice that they're not.

And somewhere in the shadows behind them – who?

Who can possibly rule if no one who wants to do it can be allowed to?

29

On a small obscure world somewhere in the middle of nowhere in particular – nowhere, that is, that could ever be found, since it is protected by a vast field of unprobability to which only six men in this galaxy have a key – it was raining.

It was bucketing down, and had been for hours. It beat the top of the sea into a mist, it pounded the trees, it churned and slopped a stretch of scrubby land near the sea into a mudbath.

The rain pelted and danced on the corrugated-iron roof of the small shack that stood in the middle of this patch of scrubby land. It obliterated the small rough pathway that led from the shack down to the seashore and smashed apart the neat piles of interesting shells which had been placed there.

The noise of the rain on the roof of the shack was deafening within, but went largely unnoticed by its occupant, whose attention was otherwise engaged.

He was a tall shambling man with rough straw-coloured hair that was damp from the leaking roof. His clothes were shabby, his back was hunched, and his eyes, though open, seemed closed.

In his shack was an old beaten-up armchair, an old scratched table, an old mattress, some cushions and a stove that was small but warm.

There was also an old and slightly weatherbeaten cat, and this was currently the focus of the man's attention. He bent his shambling form over it.

'Pussy, pussy, pussy,' he said, 'coochicoochicoochicoo ... pussy want his fish? Nice piece of fish ... pussy want it?'

The cat seemed undecided on the matter. It pawed rather condescendingly at the piece of fish the man was holding out, and then got distracted by a piece of dust on the floor.

'Pussy not eat his fish, pussy get thin and waste away, I think,' said the man. Doubt crept into his voice.

'I imagine this is what will happen,' he said, 'but how can I tell?'

He proffered the fish again.

'Pussy think,' he said, 'eat fish or not eat fish. I think it is better if I don't get involved.' He sighed.

'I think fish is nice, but then I think that rain is wet, so who am I to judge?'

He left the fish on the floor for the cat, and retired to his seat.

'Ah, I seem to see you eating it,' he said at last, as the cat exhausted the entertainment possibilities of the speck of dust and pounced on to the fish.

'I like it when I see you eat fish,' said the man, 'because in my mind you will waste away if you don't.'

He picked up from the table a piece of paper and the stub of a pencil. He held one in one hand and the other in the other, and experimented with the different ways of bringing them together. He tried holding the pencil under the paper, then over the paper, then next to the paper. He tried wrapping the paper round the pencil, he tried rubbing the stubby end of the pencil against the paper and then he tried rubbing the sharp end of the pencil against the paper. It made a mark, and he was delighted with the discovery, as he was every day. He picked up another piece of paper from the table. This had a crossword on it. He studied it briefly and filled in a couple of clues before losing interest.

He tried sitting on one of his hands and was intrigued by the feel of the bones on his hip.

'Fish come from far away,' he said, 'or so I'm told. Or so I imagine I'm told. When the men come, or when in my mind the men come in their six black shiny ships, do they come in your mind too? What do you see, pussy?'

He looked at the cat, which was more concerned with getting the fish down as rapidly as possible than it was with these speculations.

'And when I hear their questions, do you hear questions? What do their voices mean to you? Perhaps you just think they're singing songs to you.' He reflected on this, and saw the flaw in the supposition.

'Perhaps they are singing songs to you,' he said, 'and I just think they're asking me questions.'

He paused again. Sometimes he would pause for days, just to see what it was like.

'Do you think they came today?' he said. 'I do. There's mud on the floor, cigarettes and whisky on the table, fish on a plate for you and a memory of them in my mind. Hardly conclusive evidence, I know, but then all evidence is circumstantial. And look what else they've left me.'

He reached over to the table and pulled some things off it.

'Crosswords, dictionaries, and a calculator.'

He played with the calculator for an hour, whilst the cat went to sleep and the rain outside continued to pour. Eventually he put the calculator aside.

'I think I must be right in thinking they ask me questions,' he said. 'To come all that way and leave all these things just for the privilege of singing songs to you would be very strange behaviour. Or so it seems to me. Who can tell, who can tell.'

From the table he picked up a cigarette and lit it with a spill from the stove. He inhaled deeply and sat back.

'I think I saw another ship in the sky today,' he said at last. 'A big white one. I've never seen a big white one, just the six black ones. And the six green ones. And the others who say they come from so far away. Never a big white one. Perhaps six small black ones can look like one big white one at certain times. Perhaps I would like a glass of whisky. Yes, that seems more likely.'

He stood up and found a glass that was lying on the floor by his mattress. He poured in a measure from his whisky bottle. He sat again.

'Perhaps some other people are coming to see me,' he said.

A hundred yards away, pelted by the torrential rain, lay the *Heart of Gold*.

Its hatchway opened, and three figures emerged, huddling into themselves to keep the rain off their faces.

'In there?' shouted Trillian above the noise of the rain.

'Yes,' said Zarniwoop.

'That shack?'

'Yes.'

'Weird,' said Zaphod.

'But it's in the middle of nowhere,' said Trillian, 'we must have come to the wrong place. You can't rule the Universe from a shack.'

They hurried through the pouring rain, and arrived, wet through, at the door. They knocked. They shivered.

The door opened.

'Hello?' said the man.

'Ah, excuse me,' said Zarniwoop, 'I have reason to believe . . .'

'Do you rule the Universe?' said Zaphod.

The man smiled at him.

'I try not to,' he said. 'Are you wet?'

Zaphod looked at him in astonishment.

'Wet?' he cried. 'Doesn't it look as if we're wet?'

'That's how it looks to me,' said the man, 'but how you feel about it might be an altogether different matter. If you find warmth makes you dry, you'd better come in.'

They went in.

They looked around the tiny shack, Zarniwoop with slight distaste, Trillian with interest, Zaphod with delight.

'Hey, er . . .' said Zaphod, 'what's your name?'

The man looked at them doubtfully.

'I don't know. Why, do you think I should have one? It seems very odd to give a bundle of vague sensory perceptions a name.'

He invited Trillian to sit in the chair. He sat on the edge of the chair, Zarniwoop leaned stiffly against the table and Zaphod lay on the mattress.

'Wowee!' said Zaphod. 'The seat of power!' He tickled the cat.

'Listen,' said Zarniwoop, 'I must ask you some questions.'

'All right,' said the man kindly, 'you can sing to my cat if you like.'

'Would he like that?' asked Zaphod.

'You'd better ask him,' said the man.

'Does he talk?' said Zaphod.

'I have no memory of him talking,' said the man, 'but I am very unreliable.'

Zarniwoop pulled some notes out of a pocket.

'Now,' he said, 'you do rule the Universe, do you?'

'How can I tell?' said the man.

Zarniwoop ticked off a note on the paper.

'How long have you been doing this?'

'Ah,' said the man, 'this is a question about the past, is it?'

Zarniwoop looked at him in puzzlement. This wasn't exactly what he had been expecting.

'Yes,' he said.

'How can I tell,' said the man, 'that the past isn't a fiction designed to account for the discrepancy between my immediate physical sensations and my state of mind?'

Zarniwoop stared at him. The steam began to rise from his sodden clothes.

'So you answer all questions like this?' he said.

The man answered quickly.

'I say what it occurs to me to say when I think I hear people say things. More I cannot say.'

Zaphod laughed happily.

'I'll drink to that,' he said and pulled out the bottle of Janx Spirit. He leaped up and handed the bottle to the ruler of the Universe, who took it with pleasure.

'Good on you, great ruler,' he said, 'tell it like it is.'

'No, listen to me,' said Zarniwoop, 'people come to you, do they? In ships . . .'

'I think so,' said the man. He handed the bottle to Trillian.

'And they ask you,' said Zarniwoop, 'to take decisions for them? About people's lives, about worlds, about economies, about wars, about everything going on out there in the Universe?'

'Out there?' said the man. 'Out where?'

'Out there!' said Zarniwoop, pointing at the door.

'How can you tell there's anything out there?' said the man politely. 'The door's closed.'

The rain continued to pound the roof. Inside the shack it was warm.

'But you know there's a whole Universe out there!'

cried Zarniwoop. 'You can't dodge your responsibilities by saying they don't exist!'

The ruler of the Universe thought for a long while whilst Zarniwoop quivered with anger.

'You're very sure of your facts,' he said at last, 'I couldn't trust the thinking of a man who takes the Universe – if there is one – for granted.'

Zarniwoop still quivered, but was silent.

'I only decide about my Universe,' continued the man quietly. 'My Universe is my eyes and my ears. Anything else is hearsay.'

'But don't you believe in anything?'

The man shrugged and picked up his cat.

'I don't understand what you mean,' he said.

'You don't understand that what you decide in this shack of yours affects the lives and fates of millions of people? This is all monstrously wrong!'

'I don't know. I've never met all these people you speak of. And neither, I suspect, have you. They only exist in words we hear. It is folly to say you know what is happening to other people. Only they know, if they exist. They have their own Universes of their eyes and ears.'

Trillian said:

'I think I'm just popping outside for a moment.'

She left and walked into the rain.

'Do you believe other people exist?' insisted Zarniwoop.

'I have no opinion. How can I say?'

'I'd better see what's up with Trillian,' said Zaphod and slipped out.

Outside, he said to her:

'I think the Universe is in pretty good hands, yeah?'

'Very good,' said Trillian. They walked off into the rain.

Inside, Zarniwoop continued.

'But don't you understand that people live or die on your word?'

The ruler of the Universe waited for as long as he could. When he heard the faint sound of the ship's engines starting, he spoke to cover it.

'It's nothing to do with me,' he said, 'I am not involved with people. The Lord knows I am not a cruel man.'

'Ah!' barked Zarniwoop, 'you say "The Lord". You believe in something!'

'My cat,' said the man benignly, picking it up and stroking it. 'I call him The Lord. I am kind to him.'

'All right,' said Zarniwoop, pressing home his point, 'how do you know he exists? How do you know he knows you to be kind, or enjoys what he thinks of as your kindness?'

'I don't,' said the man with a smile, 'I have no idea. It merely pleases me to behave in a certain way to what appears to be a cat. Do you behave any differently? Please, I think I am tired.'

Zarniwoop heaved a thoroughly dissatisfied sigh and looked about.

'Where are the other two?' he said suddenly.

'What other two?' said the ruler of the Universe, settling back into his chair and refilling his whisky glass.

'Beeblebrox and the girl! The two who were here!'

'I remember no one. The past is a fiction to account for . . .'

'Stuff it,' snapped Zarniwoop and ran out into the rain. There was no ship. The rain continued to churn the mud. There was no sign to show where the ship had been. He hollered into the rain. He turned and ran back to the shack and found it locked.

The ruler of the Universe dozed lightly in his chair. After a while he played with the pencil and the paper again and was delighted when he discovered how to make a mark with the one on the other. Various noises continued outside, but he didn't know whether they were real or not. He then talked to his table for a week to see how it would react.

30

The stars came out that night, dazzling in their brilliance and clarity. Ford and Arthur had walked more miles than they had any means of judging and finally stopped to rest. The night was cool and balmy, the air pure, the Sub-Etha Sens-O-Matic totally silent.

A wonderful stillness hung over the world, a magical calm which combined with the soft fragrances of the woods, the quiet chatter of insects and the brilliant light of the stars to soothe their jangled spirits. Even Ford Prefect, who had seen more worlds than he could count on a long afternoon, was moved to wonder if this was the most beautiful he had ever seen. All that day they had passed through rolling green hills and valleys, richly covered with grasses, wild scented flowers and tall thickly leaved trees, the sun had warmed them, light breezes had kept them cool, and Ford Prefect had checked his Sub-Etha Sens-O-Matic at less and less frequent intervals, and had exhibited less and less annoyance at its continued silence. He was beginning to think he liked it here.

Cool though the night air was they slept soundly and comfortably in the open and awoke a few hours later with the light dewfall feeling refreshed but hungry. Ford had stuffed some small rolls into his satchel at Milliways and they breakfasted off these before moving on.

So far they had wandered purely at random, but now they struck out firmly eastwards, feeling that if they were going to explore this world they should have some clear idea of where they had come from and where they were going.

Shortly before noon they had their first indication that the world they had landed on was not an uninhabited one: a half glimpsed face amongst the trees, watching them. It vanished at the moment they both saw it, but the image they were both left with was of a humanoid creature, curious to see them but not alarmed. Half an hour later they glimsped another such face, and ten minutes after that another.

A minute later they stumbled into a wide clearing and stopped short.

Before them in the middle of the clearing stood a group of about two dozen men and women. They stood still and quiet facing Ford and Arthur. Around some of the women huddled some small children and behind the group was a ramshackle array of small dwellings made of mud and branches.

Ford and Arthur held their breath.

The tallest of the men stood little over five feet high, they all stooped forward slightly, had longish arms and lowish foreheads, and clear bright eyes with which they stared intently at the strangers.

Seeing that they carried no weapons and made no move towards them, Ford and Arthur relaxed slightly.

For a while the two groups simply stared at each other, neither side making any move. The natives seemed puzzled by the intruders, and whilst they showed no sign of aggression they were quite clearly not issuing any invitations.

Nothing happened.

For a full two minutes nothing continued to happen.

After two minutes Ford decided it was time something happened.

'Hello,' he said.

The women drew their children slightly closer to them.

The men made hardly any discernible move and yet their whole disposition made it clear that the greeting was not welcome – it was not resented in any great degree, it was just not welcome.

One of the men, who had been standing slightly forward of the rest of the group and who might therefore have been their leader, stepped forward. His face was quiet and calm, almost serene.

'Ugghhhuugghhhrrrr uh uh ruh uurgh,' he said quietly.

This caught Arthur by surprise. He had grown so used to receiving an instantaneous and unconscious translation of everything he heard via the Babel fish lodged in his ear that he had ceased to be aware of it, and he was only reminded of its presence now by the fact that it didn't seem to be working. Vague shadows of meaning had flickered at the back of his mind, but there was nothing he could get any firm grasp on. He guessed, correctly as it happens, that these people had as yet evolved no more than the barest rudiments of language, and that the Babel fish was therefore powerless to help. He glanced at Ford, who was infinitely more experienced in these matters.

'I think,' said Ford out of the corner of his mouth, 'he's asking us if we'd mind walking on round the edge of the village.'

A moment later, a gesture from the man-creature seemed to confirm this.

'Ruurgggghhhh urrgggh; urgh urgh (uh ruh) rruurruuh ug,' continued the man-creature.

'The general gist,' said Ford, 'as far as I can make out, is that we are welcome to continue our journey in any way we like, but if we would walk round his village rather than through it it would make them all very happy.'

'So what do we do?'

'I think we make them happy,' said Ford.

Slowly and watchfully they walked round the perimeter of the clearing. This seemed to go down very well with the natives who bowed to them very slightly and then went about their business.

Ford and Arthur continued their journey through the wood. A few hundred yards past the clearing they suddenly came upon a small pile of fruit lying in their path – berries that looked remarkably like raspberries and blackberries, and pulpy, green-skinned fruit that looked remarkably like pears.

So far they had steered clear of the fruit and berries they had seen, though the trees and bushes were laden with them.

'Look at it this way,' Ford Prefect had said, 'fruit and berries on strange planets either make you live or make you die. Therefore the point at which to start toying with them is when you're going to die if you don't. That way you stay ahead. The secret of healthy hitch hiking is to eat junk food.'

They looked at the pile that lay in their path with suspicion. It looked so good it made them almost dizzy with hunger.

'Look at it this way,' said Ford, 'er . . .'

'Yes?' said Arthur.

'I'm trying to think of a way of looking at it which means we get to eat it,' said Ford.

The leaf-dappled sun gleamed on the plump skins of the things which looked like pears. The things which looked like raspberries and strawberries were fatter and riper than any Arthur had ever seen, even in ice-cream commercials.

'Why don't we eat them and think about it afterwards?' he said.

'Maybe that's what they want us to do.'

'All right, look at it this way . . .'

'Sounds good so far.'

'It's there for us to eat. Either it's good or it's bad, either they want to feed us or to poison us. If it's poisonous and we don't eat it they'll just attack us some other way. If we don't eat, we lose out either way.'

'I like the way you're thinking,' said Ford. 'Now eat one.'

Hesitantly, Arthur picked up one of the things that looked like pears.

'I always thought that about the Garden of Eden story,' said Ford.

'Eh?'

'Garden of Eden. Tree. Apple. That bit, remember?'

'Yes of course I do.'

'Your God person puts an apple tree in the middle of a garden and says, "do what you like guys, oh, but don't eat the apple." Surprise surprise, they eat it and he leaps out from behind a bush shouting "Gotcha". It wouldn't have made any difference if they hadn't eaten it.'

'Why not?'

'Because if you're dealing with somebody who has the sort of mentality which likes leaving hats on the pavement with bricks under them you know perfectly well they won't give up. They'll get you in the end.'

'What are you talking about?'

'Never mind, eat the fruit.'

'You know, this place almost looks like the Garden of Eden.'

'Eat the fruit.'

'Sounds quite like it too.'

Arthur took a bite from the thing which looked like a pear.

'It's a pear,' he said.

A few moments later, when they had eaten the lot, Ford Prefect turned round and called out.

'Thank you. Thank you very much,' he called, 'you're very kind.'

They went on their way.

For the next fifty miles of their journey eastward they kept on finding the occasional gift of fruit lying in their path, and though they once or twice had a quick glimpse of a native man-creature amongst the trees, they never again made direct contact. They decided they rather liked a race of people who made it clear that they were grateful simply to be left alone.

The fruit and berries stopped after fifty miles, because that was where the sea started.

Having no pressing calls on their time they built a raft and crossed the sea. It was relatively calm, only about sixty miles wide and they had a reasonably pleasant crossing, landing in a country that was at least as beautiful as the one they had left.

Life was, in short, ridiculously easy and for a while at least they were able to cope with the problems of aimlessness and isolation by deciding to ignore them. When the craving for company became too great they would know where to find it, but for the moment they were happy to feel that the Golgafrinchans were hundreds of miles behind them.

Nevertheless, Ford Prefect began to use his Sub-Etha Sens-O-Matic more often again. Only once did he pick up a signal, but that was so faint and from such enormous distance that it depressed him more than the silence that had otherwise continued unbroken.

On a whim they turned northwards. After weeks of travelling they came to another sea, built another raft and crossed it. This time it was harder going, the climate was getting colder. Arthur suspected a streak of masochism in Ford Prefect – the increasing difficulty of the journey seemed to give him a sense of purpose that was otherwise lacking. He strode onwards relentlessly.

Their journey northwards brought them into steep mountainous terrain of breathtaking sweep and beauty. The vast, jagged, snow-covered peaks ravished their senses. The cold began to bite into their bones.

They wrapped themselves in animal skins and furs which Ford Prefect acquired by a technique he once learned from a couple of ex-Pralite monks running a Mind-Surfing resort in the Hills of Hunian.

The Galaxy is littered with ex-Pralite monks, all on the make, because the mental-control techniques the Order has evolved as a form of devotional discipline are, frankly, sensational – and extraordinary numbers of monks leave the Order just after they have finished their devotional training and just before they take their final vows to stay locked in small metal boxes for the rest of their lives.

Ford's technique seemed to consist mainly of standing still for a while and smiling.

After a while an animal – a deer perhaps – would appear from out of the trees and watch him cautiously. Ford would continue to smile at it, his eyes would soften and shine, and he would seem to radiate a deep and universal love, a love which reached out to embrace all of creation. A wonderful quietness would descend on the surrounding countryside, peaceful and serene, emanating from this transfigured man. Slowly the deer would approach, step by step, until it was almost nuzzling him, whereupon Ford Prefect would reach out to it and break its neck.

'Pheromone control,' he said it was, 'you just have to know how to generate the right smell.'

31

A few days after landing in this mountainous land they hit a coastline which swept diagonally before them from the south-west to the north-east, a coastline of monumental grandeur: deep majestic ravines, soaring pinnacles of ice – fjords.

For two further days they scrambled and climbed over the rocks and glaciers, awe-struck with beauty.

'Arthur!' yelled Ford suddenly.

It was the afternoon of the second day. Arthur was sitting on a high rock watching the thundering sea smashing itself against the craggy promontories.

'Arthur!' yelled Ford again.

Arthur looked to where Ford's voice had come from, carried faintly in the wind.

Ford had gone to examine a glacier, and Arthur found him there crouching by the solid wall of blue ice. He was tense with excitement – his eyes darted up to meet Arthur's.

'Look,' he said, 'look!'

Arthur looked. He saw the solid wall of blue ice.

'Yes,' he said, 'it's a glacier. I've already seen it.'

'No,' said Ford, 'you've looked at it, you haven't seen it. Look.'

Ford was pointing deep into the heart of the ice.

Arthur peered – he saw nothing but vague shadows.

'Move back from it,' insisted Ford, 'look again.'

Arthur moved back and looked again.

'No,' he said, and shrugged. 'What am I supposed to be looking for?'

And suddenly he saw it.

'You see it?'

He saw it.

His mouth started to speak, but his brain decided it hadn't got anything to say yet and shut it again. His brain then started to contend with the problem of what his eyes told it they were looking at, but in doing so relinquished control of the mouth which promptly fell open again. Once more gathering up the jaw, his brain lost control of his left hand which then wandered around in an aimless fashion. For a second or so the brain tried to catch the left hand without letting go of the mouth and simultaneously tried to think about what was buried in the ice, which is probably why the legs went and Arthur dropped restfully to the ground.

The thing that had been causing all this neural upset was a network of shadows in the ice, about eighteen inches beneath the surface. Looked at from the right angle they resolved into the solid shapes of letters from an alien alphabet, each about three feet high; and for those, like Arthur, who couldn't read Magrathean there was above the letters the outline of a face hanging in the ice.

It was an old face, thin and distinguished, careworn but not unkind.

It was the face of the man who had won an award for designing the coastline they now knew themselves to be standing on.

32

A thin whine filled the air. It whirled and howled through the trees upsetting the squirrels. A few birds flew off in disgust. The noise danced and skittered round the clearing. It whooped, it rasped, it generally offended.

The captain, however, regarded the lone bagpiper with an indulgent eye. Little could disturb his equanimity; indeed, once he had got over the loss of his gorgeous bath during that unpleasantness in the swamp all those months ago he had begun to find his new life remarkably congenial. A hollow had been scooped out of a large rock which stood in the middle of the clearing, and in this he would bask daily whilst attendants sloshed water over him. Not particularly warm water, it must be said, as they hadn't yet worked out a way of heating it. Never mind, that would come, and in the meantime search parties were scouring the countryside far and wide for a hot spring, preferably one in a nice leafy glade, and if it was near a soap mine – perfection. To those who said that they had a feeling soap wasn't found in mines, the captain had ventured to suggest that perhaps that was because no one had looked hard enough, and this possibility had been reluctantly acknowledged.

No, life was very pleasant, and the great thing about it was that when the hot spring was found, complete with leafy glade *en suite*, and when in the fulness of time the cry came reverberating across the hills that the soap mine had been located and was producing five hundred cakes a day it would be more pleasant still. It was very important to have things to look forward to.

Wail, wail, screech, wail, howl, honk, squeak went the bagpipes, increasing the captain's already considerable pleasure at the thought that any moment now they might stop. That was something he looked forward to as well.

What else was pleasant, he asked himself? Well, so many things: the red and gold of the trees, now that autumn was approaching; the peaceful chatter of scissors a few feet from his bath where a couple of hairdressers were exercising their skills on a dozing art director and his assistant; the sunlight gleaming off the six shiny telephones lined up along the edge of his rock-hewn bath. The only thing nicer than a phone that didn't ring all the time (or indeed at all) was six phones that didn't ring all the time (or indeed at all).

Nicest of all was the happy murmur of all the hundreds of people slowly assembling in the clearing around him to watch the afternoon committee meeting.

The captain punched his rubber duck playfully on the beak. The afternoon committee meetings were his favourite.

Other eyes watched the assembling crowds. High in a tree on the edge of the clearing squatted Ford Prefect, lately returned from foreign climes. After his six-month journey he was lean and healthy, his eyes gleamed, he wore a reindeer-skin coat; his beard was as thick and his face as bronzed as a country-rock singer's.

He and Arthur Dent had been watching the Golgafrinchans for almost a week now, and Ford had decided it was time to stir things up a bit.

The clearing was now full. Hundreds of men and women lounged around, chatting, eating fruit, playing cards and generally having a fairly relaxed time of it. Their track suits were now all dirty and even torn, but they all had immaculately styled hair. Ford was puzzled to see that many of them had stuffed their track suits full of leaves and wondered if this was meant to be some form of insulation against the coming winter. Ford's eyes narrowed. They couldn't be interested in botany of a sudden, could they?

In the middle of these speculations the captain's voice rose above the hubbub.

'All right,' he said, 'I'd like to call this meeting to some sort of order if that's at all possible. Is that all right with everybody?' He smiled genially. 'In a minute. When you're all ready.'

The talking gradually died away and the clearing fell silent, except for the bagpiper who seemed to be in some wild and uninhabitable musical world of his own. A few of those in his immediate vicinity threw some leaves to him. If there was any reason for this then it escaped Ford Prefect for the moment.

A small group of people had clustered round the captain and one of them was clearly preparing to speak. He did this by standing up, clearing his throat and then gazing off into the distance as if to signify to the crowd that he would be with them in a minute.

The crowd of course were riveted and all turned their eyes on him.

A moment of silence followed, which Ford judged to be the right dramatic moment to make his entry. The man turned to speak.

Ford dropped down out of the tree.

'Hi there,' he said.

The crowd swivelled round.

'Ah, my dear fellow,' called out the captain. 'Got any matches on you? Or a lighter? Anything like that?'

'No,' said Ford, sounding a little deflated. It wasn't what he'd prepared. He decided he'd better be a little stronger on the subject.

'No I haven't,' he continued. 'No matches. Instead I bring you news . . .'

'Pity,' said the captain. 'We've all run out, you see. Haven't had a hot bath in weeks.'

Ford refused to be headed off.

'I bring you news,' he said, 'of a discovery that might interest you.'

'Is it on the agenda?' snapped the man whom Ford had interrupted.

Ford smiled a broad country-rock singer smile.

'Now, come on,' he said.

'Well I'm sorry,' said the man huffily, 'but speaking as a management consultant of many years' standing, I must insist on the importance of observing the committee structure.'

Ford looked round the crowd.

'He's mad, you know,' he said, 'this is a prehistoric planet.'

'Address the chair!' snapped the management consultant.

'There isn't a chair,' explained Ford, 'there's only a rock.'

The management consultant decided that testiness was what the situation now called for.

'Well, call it a chair,' he said testily.

'Why not call it a rock?' asked Ford.

'You obviously have no conception,' said the management consultant, now abandoning testiness in favour of good old-fashioned hauteur, 'of modern business methods.'

'And you have no conception of where you are,' said Ford.

A girl with a strident voice leapt to her feet and used it.

'Shut up, you two,' she said, 'I want to table a motion.'

'You mean boulder a motion,' tittered a hairdresser.

'Order, order!' yapped the management consultant.

'All right,' said Ford, 'let's see how you're doing.' He plonked himself down on the ground to see how long he could keep his temper.

The captain made a sort of conciliatory harrumphing noise.

'I would like to call to order,' he said pleasantly, 'the five-hundred and seventy-third meeting of the colonization committee of Fintlewoodlewix . . .'

Ten seconds, thought Ford as he leapt to his feet again.

'This is futile,' he exclaimed, 'five hundred and seventy-three committee meetings and you haven't even discovered fire yet!'

'If you would care,' said the girl with the strident voice, 'to examine the agenda sheet . . .'

'Agenda rock,' trilled the hairdresser happily.

'Thank you, I've made that point,' muttered Ford.

'. . . you . . . will . . . see . . .' continued the girl firmly, 'that we are having a report from the Hairdressers' Fire Development Sub-Committee today.'

'Oh . . . ah – ' said the hairdresser with a sheepish look which is recognized the whole Galaxy over as meaning, 'Er, will next Tuesday do?'

'All right,' said Ford, rounding on him, 'what have you done? What are you going to do? What are your thoughts on fire development?'

'Well, I don't know,' said the hairdresser. 'All they gave me was a couple of sticks . . .'

'So what have you done with them?'

Nervously, the hairdresser fished in his track-suit top and handed over the fruits of his labour to Ford.

Ford held them up for all to see.

'Curling tongs,' he said.

The crowd applauded.

'Never mind,' said Ford. 'Rome wasn't burnt in a day.'

The crowd hadn't the faintest idea what he was talking about, but they loved it nevertheless. They applauded.

'Well, you're obviously being totally naive, of course,' said the girl. 'When you've been in marketing as long as I have you'll know that before any new product can be developed it has to be properly researched. We've got to find out what people want from fire, how they relate to it, what sort of image it has for them.'

The crowd were tense. They were expecting something wonderful from Ford.

'Stick it up your nose,' he said.

'Which is precisely the sort of thing we need to know,' insisted the girl. 'Do people want fire that can be fitted nasally?'

'Do you?' Ford asked the crowd.

'Yes!' shouted some.

'No!' shouted others happily.

They didn't know, they just thought it was great.

'And the wheel,' said the captain. 'What about this wheel thingy? It sounds a terribly interesting project.'

'Ah,' said the marketing girl, 'well, we're having a little difficulty there.'

'Difficulty?' exclaimed Ford. 'Difficulty? What do you mean, difficulty? It's the single simplest machine in the entire Universe!'

The marketing girl soured him with a look.

'All right, Mr Wiseguy,' she said, 'you're so clever, you tell us what colour it should be.'

The crowd went wild. One up to the home team, they thought. Ford shrugged his shoulders and sat down again.

'Almighty Zarquon,' he said, 'have none of you done anything?'

As if in answer to his question there was a sudden clamour of noise from the entrance to the clearing. The crowd couldn't believe the amount of entertainment they were getting this afternoon: in marched a squad of about a dozen men dressed in the remnants of their Golgafrinchan 3rd Regiment dress uniforms. About half of them still carried Kill-O-Zap guns, the rest now carried spears which they struck together as they marched. They looked bronzed, healthy and utterly exhausted and bedraggled. They clattered to a halt and banged to attention. One of them fell over and never moved again.

'Captain, sir!' cried Number Two – for he was their leader – 'Permission to report, sir!'

'Yes, all right Number Two, welcome back and all that. Find any hot springs?' said the captain despondently.

'No, sir!'

'Thought you wouldn't.'

Number Two strode through the crowd and presented arms before the bath.

'We have discovered another continent!'

'When was this?'

'It lies across the sea . . .' said Number Two, narrowing his eyes significantly, 'to the east!'

'Ah.'

Number Two turned to face the crowd. He raised his gun above his head. This is going to be great, thought the crowd.

'We have declared war on it!'

Wild abandoned cheering broke out in all corners of the clearing – this was beyond all expectation.

'Wait a minute,' shouted Ford Prefect, 'wait a minute!'

He leapt to his feet and demanded silence. After a

while he got it, or at least the best silence he could hope for under the circumstances: the circumstances were that the bagpiper was spontaneously composing a national anthem.

'Do we have to have the piper?' demanded Ford.

'Oh yes,' said the captain, 'we've given him a grant.'

Ford considered opening this idea up for debate but quickly decided that that way madness lay. Instead he slung a well-judged rock at the piper and turned to face Number Two.

'War?' he said.

'Yes!' Number Two gazed contemptuously at Ford Prefect.

'On the next continent?'

'Yes! Total warfare! The war to end all wars!'

'But there's no one even living there yet!'

Ah, interesting, thought the crowd, nice point.

Number Two's gaze hovered undisturbed. In this respect his eyes were like a couple of mosquitos that hover purposefully three inches from your nose and refuse to be deflected by arm thrashes, fly swats or rolled newspapers.

'I know that,' he said, 'but there will be one day! So we have left an open-ended ultimatum.'

'What?'

'And blown up a few military installations.'

The captain leaned forward out of his bath.

'Military installations, Number Two?' he said.

For a moment the eyes wavered.

'Yes, sir, well, potential military installations. All right . . . trees.'

The moment of uncertainty passed – his eyes flicked like whips over his audience.

'And,' he roared, 'we interrogated a gazelle!'

He flipped his Kill-O-Zap smartly under his arm and marched off through the pandemonium that had now erupted throughout the ecstatic crowd. A few steps was all he managed before he was caught up and carried shoulder high for a lap of honour round the clearing.

Ford sat and idly tapped a couple of stones together.

'So what else have you done?' he enquired after the celebrations had died down.

'We have started a culture,' said the marketing girl.

'Oh yes?' said Ford.

'Yes. One of our film producers is already making a fascinating documentary about the indeginous cavemen of the area.'

'They're not cavemen.'

'They look like cavemen.'

'Do they live in caves?'

'Well . . .'

'They live in huts.'

'Perhaps they're having their caves redecorated,' called out a wag from the crowd.

Ford rounded on him angrily.

'Very funny,' he said, 'but have you noticed that they're dying out?'

On their journey back, Ford and Arthur had come across two derelict villages and the bodies of many natives in the woods, where they had crept away to die. Those that still lived seemed stricken and listless, as if they were suffering from some disease of the spirit rather than the body. They moved sluggishly and with an infinite sadness. Their future had been taken away from them.

'Dying out!' repeated Ford. 'Do you know what that means?'

'Er . . . we shouldn't sell them any life insurance?' called out the wag again.

Ford ignored him, and appealed to the whole crowd.

'Can you try and understand,' he said, 'that it's just since we've arrived here that they've started dying out!'

'In fact that comes over terribly well in this film,' said the marketing girl, 'and just gives it that poignant twist which is the hallmark of the really great documentary. The producer's very committed.'

'He should be,' muttered Ford.

'I gather,' said the girl, turning to address the captain, who was beginning to nod off, 'that he wants to make one about you next, Captain.'

'Oh really?' he said, coming to with a start. 'That's awfully nice.'

'He's got a very strong angle on it, you know, the burden of responsibility, the loneliness of command . . .'

The captain hummed and hahed about this for a moment.

'Well, I wouldn't overstress that angle, you know,' he said finally, 'one's never alone with a rubber duck.'

He held the duck aloft and it got an appreciative round from the crowd.

All this while, the management consultant had been sitting in stony silence, his fingertips pressed to his temples to indicate that he was waiting and would wait all day if it was necessary.

At this point he decided he would not wait all day after all, he would merely pretend that the last half hour hadn't happened.

He rose to his feet.

'If,' he said tersely, 'we could for a moment move on to the subject of fiscal policy . . .'

'Fiscal policy!' whooped Ford Prefect. 'Fiscal policy!'

The management consultant gave him a look that only a lungfish could have copied.

'Fiscal policy . . .' he repeated, 'that is what I said.'

'How can you have money,' demanded Ford, 'if none of you actually produces anything? It doesn't grow on trees, you know.'

'If you would allow me to continue . . .'

Ford nodded dejectedly.

'Thank you. Since we decided a few weeks ago to adopt the leaf as legal tender, we have, of course, all become immensely rich.'

Ford stared in disbelief at the crowd who were murmuring appreciatively at this and greedily fingering the wads of leaves with which their track suits were stuffed.

'But we have also,' continued the management consultant, 'run into a small inflation problem on account of the high level of leaf availability, which means that, I gather, the current going rate has something like three deciduous forests buying one ship's peanut.'

Murmurs of alarm came from the crowd. The management consultant waved them down.

'So in order to obviate this problem,' he continued, 'and effectively revalue the leaf, we are about to embark on a massive defoliation campaign, and . . . er, burn down all the forests. I think you'll all agree that's a sensible move under the circumstances.'

The crowd seemed a little uncertain about this for a second or two until someone pointed out how much this would increase the value of the leaves in their pockets whereupon they let out whoops of delight and gave the management consultant a standing ovation. The accountants amongst them looked forward to a profitable autumn.

'You're all mad,' explained Ford Prefect.

'You're absolutely barmy,' he suggested.

'You're a bunch of raving nutters,' he opined.

The tide of opinion was beginning to turn against him. What had started out as excellent entertainment had now, in the crowd's view, deteriorated into mere abuse, and since this abuse was in the main directed at them they wearied of it.

Sensing this shift in the wind, the marketing girl turned on him.

'Is it perhaps in order,' she demanded, 'to enquire what you've been doing all these months, then? You and that other interloper have been missing since the day we arrived.'

'We've been on a journey,' said Ford. 'We went to try and find out something about this planet.'

'Oh,' said the girl archly, 'doesn't sound very productive to me.'

'No? Well have I got news for you, my love. We have discovered this planet's future.'

Ford waited for this statement to have its effect. It didn't have any. They didn't know what he was talking about.

He continued.

'It doesn't matter a pair of fetid dingo's kidneys what you all choose to do from now on. Burn down the forests, anything, it won't make a scrap of difference. Your future history has already happened. Two million years you've got and that's it. At the end of that time your race will be dead, gone and good riddance to you. Remember that, two million years!'

The crowd muttered to itself in annoyance. People as rich as they had suddenly become shouldn't be obliged to listen to this sort of gibberish. Perhaps they could tip the fellow a leaf or two and he would go away.

They didn't need to bother. Ford was already stalking out of the clearing, pausing only to shake his head at Number Two, who was already firing his Kill-O-Zap into some neighbouring trees.

He turned back once.

'Two million years!' he said and laughed.

'Well,' said the captain with a soothing smile, 'still time for a few more baths. Could someone pass me the sponge? I just dropped it over the side.'

33

A mile or so away through the wood, Arthur Dent was too busily engrossed with what he was doing to hear Ford Prefect approach.

What he was doing was rather curious, and this is what it was: on a wide flat piece of rock he had scratched out the shape of a large square, subdivided into one hundred and sixty-nine smaller squares, thirteen to a side.

Furthermore he had collected together a pile of smallish flattish stones and scratched the shape of a letter on to each. Sitting morosely round the rock were a couple of the surviving local native men to whom Arthur Dent was trying to introduce the curious concept embodied in these stones.

So far they had not done well. They had attempted to eat some of them, bury others and throw the rest of them away. Arthur had finally encouraged one of them to lay a couple of stones on the board he had scratched out, which was not even as far as he'd managed to get the day before. Along with the rapid deterioration in the morale of these creatures, there seemed to be a corresponding deterioration in their actual intelligence.

In an attempt to egg them along, Arthur set out a number of letters on the board himself, and then tried to encourage the natives to add some more themselves.

It was not going well.

Ford watched quietly from beside a nearby tree.

'No,' said Arthur to one of the natives who had just shuffled some of the letters round in a fit of abysmal dejection, 'Q scores ten you see, and it's on a triple word score, so ... Look, I've explained the rules to you ... No, no, look, please, put down that jawbone ...

All right, we'll start again. And try to concentrate this time.'

Ford leaned his elbow against the tree and his hand against his head.

'What are you doing, Arthur?' he asked quietly.

Arthur looked up with a start. He suddenly had a feeling that all this might look slightly foolish. All he knew was that it had worked like a dream on him when he was a child. But things were different then, or rather would be.

'I'm trying to teach the cavemen to play Scrabble,' he said.

'They're not cavemen,' said Ford.

'They look like cavemen.'

Ford let it pass.

'I see,' he said.

'It's uphill work,' said Arthur wearily, 'the only word they know is grunt and they can't spell it.'

He sighed and sat back.

'What's that supposed to achieve?' asked Ford.

'We've got to encourage them to evolve! To develop!' Arthur burst out angrily. He hoped that the weary sigh and then the anger might do something to counteract the overriding feeling of foolishness from which he was currently suffering. It didn't. He jumped to his feet.

'Can you imagine what a world would be like descended from those . . . cretins we arrived with?' he said.

'Imagine?' said Ford, raising his eyebrows. 'We don't have to imagine. We've seen it.'

'But . . .' Arthur waved his arms about hopelessly.

'We've seen it,' said Ford, 'there's no escape.'

Arthur kicked at a stone.

'Did you tell them what we'd discovered?' he asked.

'Hmmmm?' said Ford, not really concentrating.

'Norway,' said Arthur. 'Slartibartfast's signature in the glacier. Did you tell them?'

'What's the point?' said Ford. 'What would it mean to them?'

'Mean?' said Arthur. 'Mean? You know perfectly well what it means. It means that this planet is the Earth! It's my home! It's where I was born!'

'Was?' said Ford.

'All right, will be.'

'Yes, in two million years' time. Why don't you tell them that? Go and say to them, "Excuse me, I'd just like to point out that in two million years' time I will be born just a few miles from here." See what they say. They'll chase you up a tree and set fire to it.'

Arthur absorbed this unhappily.

'Face it,' said Ford, 'those zeebs over there are your ancestors, not these poor creatures here.'

He went over to where the apemen creatures were rummaging listlessly with the stone letters. He shook his head.

'Put the Scrabble away, Arthur,' he said, 'it won't save the human race, because this lot aren't going to be the human race. The human race is currently sitting round a rock on the other side of this hill making documentaries about themselves.'

Arthur winced.

'There must be something we can do,' he said. A terrible sense of desolation thrilled through his body that he should be here, on the Earth, the Earth which had lost its future in a horrifying arbitrary catastrophe and which now seemed set to lose its past as well.

'No,' said Ford, 'there's nothing we can do. This doesn't change the history of the Earth, you see, this *is* the history of the Earth. Like it or leave it, the Golgafrinchans are the people you are descended from. In two million years they get destroyed by the Vogons. History is never altered you see, it just fits together like a jigsaw. Funny old thing, life, isn't it?'

He picked up the letter Q and hurled it into a distant privet bush where it hit a young rabbit. The rabbit hurtled off in terror and didn't stop till it was set upon and eaten by a fox which choked on one of its bones and died on the bank of a stream which subsequently washed it away.

During the following weeks Ford Prefect swallowed his pride and struck up a relationship with a girl who had been a personnel officer on Golgafrinchan, and he was terribly upset when she suddenly passed away as a result of drinking water from a pool that had been polluted by the body of a dead fox. The only moral it is possible to draw from this story is that one should never throw the letter Q into a privet bush, but unfortunately there are times when it is unavoidable.

Like most of the really crucial things in life, this chain of events was completely invisible to Ford Prefect and Arthur Dent. They were looking sadly at one of the natives morosely pushing the other letters around.

'Poor bloody caveman,' said Arthur.

'They're not . . .'

'What?'

'Oh, never mind,' said Ford.

The wretched creature let out a pathetic howling noise and banged on the rock.

'It's all been a bit of a waste of time for them, hasn't it?' said Arthur.

'Uh uh urghhhhh,' muttered the native and banged on the rock again.

'They've been out-evolved by telephone sanitizers.'

'Urgh, grr grr, gruh!' insisted the native, continuing to bang on the rock.

'Why does he keep banging on the rock?' said Arthur.

'I think he probably wants you to Scrabble with him again,' said Ford, 'he's pointing to the letters.'

'Probably spelt crzjgrdwldiwdc again, poor bastard. I keep on telling him there's only one g in crzjgrdwldiwdc.'

The native banged on the rock again.

They looked over his shoulder.

Their eyes popped.

There amongst the jumble of letters were eight that had been laid out in a clear straight line.

They spelt two words.

The words were these:

'FORTY-TWO.'

'Grrrurgh guh guh,' explained the native. He swept the letters angrily away and went and mooched under a nearby tree with his colleague.

Ford and Arthur stared at him. Then they stared at each other.

'Did that say what I thought it said?' they both said to each other.

'Yes,' they both said.

'Forty-two,' said Arthur.

'Forty-two,' said Ford.

Arthur ran over to the two natives.

'What are you trying to tell us?' he shouted. 'What's it supposed to mean?'

One of them rolled over on the ground, kicked his legs up in the air, rolled over again and went to sleep.

The other bounded up the tree and threw horse chestnuts at Ford Prefect. Whatever it was they had to say, they had already said it.

'You know what this means,' said Ford.

'Not entirely.'

'Forty-two is the number Deep Thought gave as being the Ultimate Answer.'

'Yes.'

'And the Earth is the computer Deep Thought designed and built to calculate the Question to the Ultimate Answer.'

'So we are led to believe.'

'And organic life was part of the computer matrix.'

'If you say so.'

'I do say so. That means that these natives, these apemen, are an integral part of the computer program, and that we and the Golgafrinchans are *not*.'

'But the cavemen are dying out and the Golgafrinchans are obviously set to replace them.'

'Exactly. So you do see what this means.'

'What?'

'Cock-up,' said Ford Prefect.

Arthur looked around him.

'This planet is having a pretty bloody time of it,' he said.

Ford puzzled for a moment.

'Still, something must have come out of it,' he said at last, 'because Marvin said he could see the Question printed in your brain-wave patterns.'

'But . . .'

'Probably the wrong one, or a distortion of the right one. It might give us a clue, though, if we could find it. I don't see how we can, though.'

They moped about for a bit. Arthur sat on the ground and started pulling up bits of grass, but found that it wasn't an occupation he could get deeply engrossed in. It wasn't grass he could believe in, the trees seemed pointless, the rolling hills seemed to be rolling to nowhere and the future seemed just a tunnel to be crawled through.

Ford fiddled with his Sub-Etha Sens-O-Matic. It was silent. He sighed and put it away.

Arthur picked up one of the letter stones from his

home-made Scrabble set. It was a T. He sighed and put it down again. The letter he put it down next to was an I. That spelt IT. He tossed another couple of letters next to them. They were an S and an H, as it happened. By a curious coincidence the resulting word perfectly expressed the way Arthur was feeling about things just then. He stared at it for a moment. He hadn't done it deliberately, it was just a random chance. His brain got slowly into first gear.

'Ford,' he said suddenly, 'look, if that Question is printed in my brain-wave patterns but I'm not consciously aware of it it must be somewhere in my unconscious.'

'Yes, I suppose so.'

'There might be a way of bringing that unconscious pattern forward.'

'Oh yes?'

'Yes, by introducing some random element that can be shaped by that pattern.'

'Like how?'

'Like by pulling Scrabble letters out of a bag blindfold.'

Ford leapt to his feet.

'Brilliant!' he said. He tugged his towel out of his satchel and with a few deft knots transformed it into a bag.

'Totally mad,' he said, 'utter nonsense. But we'll do it because it's brilliant nonsense. Come on, come on.'

The sun passed respectfully behind a cloud. A few small sad raindrops fell.

They piled together all the remaining letters and dropped them into the bag. They shook them up.

'Right,' said Ford, 'close your eyes. Pull them out. Come on come on, come on.'

Arthur closed his eyes and plunged his hand into the towelful of stones. He jiggled them about, pulled out four and handed them to Ford. Ford laid them along the ground in the order he got them.

'W,' said Ford, 'H, A, T . . . What!'

He blinked.

'I think it's working!' he said.

Arthur pushed three more at him.

'D, O, Y, . . . Doy. Oh perhaps it isn't working,' said Ford.

'Here's the next three.'

'O, U, G . . . Doyoug . . . It's not making sense, I'm afraid.'

Arthur pulled another two from the bag. Ford put them in place.

'E, T, doyouget . . . Do you get!' shouted Ford. 'It is working! This is amazing, it really is working!'

'More here.' Arthur was throwing them out feverishly as fast as he could go.

'I, F,' said Ford, 'Y, O, U, . . . M, U, L, T, I, P, L, Y, . . . What do you get if you multiply, . . . S, I, X, . . . six, . . . B, Y, by, six by . . . what do you get if you multiply six by . . . N, I, N, E, . . . six by nine . . .' He paused. 'Come on, where's the next one?'

'Er, that's the lot,' said Arthur, 'that's all there were.'

He sat back, nonplussed.

He rooted around again in the knotted-up towel but there were no more letters.

'You mean that's it?' said Ford.

'That's it.'

'Six by nine. Forty-two.'

'That's it. That's all there is.'

34

The sun came out and beamed cheerfully at them. A bird sang. A warm breeze wafted through the trees and lifted the heads of the flowers, carrying their scent away through the woods. An insect droned past on its way to do whatever it is that insects do in the late afternoon. The sound of voices lilted through the trees followed a moment later by two girls who stopped in surprise at the sight of Ford Prefect and Arthur Dent apparently lying on the ground in agony, but in fact rocking with noiseless laughter.

'No, don't go,' called Ford Prefect between gasps, 'we'll be with you in just a moment.'

'What's the matter?' asked one of the girls. She was the taller and slimmer of the two. On Golgafrinchan she had been a junior personnel officer, but hadn't liked it much.

Ford pulled himself together.

'Excuse me,' he said, 'hello. My friend and I were just contemplating the meaning of life. Frivolous exercise.'

'Oh, it's you,' said the girl, 'you made a bit of a spectacle of yourself this afternoon. You were quite funny to begin with but you did bang on a bit.'

'Did I? Oh yes.'

'Yes, what was all that for?' asked the other girl, a shorter round-faced girl who had been an art director for a small advertising company on Golgafrinchan. Whatever the privations of this world were, she went to sleep every night profoundly grateful for the fact that whatever she had to face in the morning it wouldn't be a hundred almost identical photographs of moodily lit tubes of toothpaste.

'For? For nothing. Nothing's *for* anything,' said Ford

Prefect happily. 'Come and join us, I'm Ford, this is Arthur. We were just about to do nothing at all for a while but it can wait.'

The girls looked at them doubtfully.

'I'm Agda,' said the tall one, 'this is Mella.'

'Hello, Agda, hello, Mella,' said Ford.

'Do you talk at all?' said Mella to Arthur.

'Oh, eventually,' said Arthur with a smile, 'but not as much as Ford.'

'Good.'

There was a slight pause.

'What did you mean,' asked Agda, 'about only having two million years? I couldn't make sense of what you were saying.'

'Oh that,' said Ford, 'doesn't matter.'

'It's just that the world gets demolished to make way for a hyperspace bypass,' said Arthur with a shrug, 'but that's two million years away, and anyway it's just Vogons doing what Vogons do.'

'Vogons?' said Mella.

'Yes, you wouldn't know them.'

'Where'd you get this idea from?'

'It really doesn't matter. It's just like a dream from the past, or the future.' Arthur smiled and looked away.

'Does it worry you that you don't talk any kind of sense?' asked Agda.

'Listen, forget it,' said Ford, 'forget all of it. Nothing matters. Look, it's a beautiful day, enjoy it. The sun, the green of the hills, the river down in the valley, the burning trees.'

'Even if it's only a dream, it's a pretty horrible idea,' said Mella, 'destroying a world just to make a bypass.'

'Oh, I've heard of worse,' said Ford, 'I read of one planet off in the seventh dimension that got used as a ball in a game of intergalactic bar billiards. Got potted straight into a black hole. Killed ten billion people.'

'That's mad,' said Mella.

'Yes, only scored thirty points too.'

Agda and Mella exchanged glances.

'Look,' said Agda, 'there's a party after the committee meeting tonight. You can come along if you like.'

'Yeah, OK,' said Ford.

'I'd like to,' said Arthur.

Many hours later Arthur and Mella sat and watched the moon rise over the dull red glow of the trees.

'That story about the world being destroyed . . .' began Mella.

'In two million years, yes.'

'You say it as if you really think it's true.'

'Yes, I think it is. I think I was there.'

She shook her head in puzzlement.

'You're very strange,' she said.

'No, I'm very ordinary,' said Arthur, 'but some very strange things have happened to me. You could say I'm more differed from than differing.'

'And that other world your friend talked about, the one that got pushed into a black hole.'

'Ah, that I don't know about. It sounds like something from the book.'

'What book?'

Arthur paused.

'*The Hitchhiker's Guide to the Galaxy*,' he said at last.

'What's that?'

'Oh, just something I threw into the river this evening. I don't think I'll be wanting it any more,' said Arthur Dent.